'Would you li

Kirsty went on, '(
salad with more o

'Nothing I'd like better,' Grant said immediately, and smiled at her in a way that suddenly made him look years younger—almost boyish, in fact, as his dark eyes looked straight into hers.

Kirsty took a quick breath, almost a gasp. What was happening? She was merely fixing a routine meal for the staff, which now seemed to include the new director, but so what? Nothing to it, and certainly not the faintest excuse for feeling as if she had taken off wildly into a state of brilliant promise and surging excitement.

After several years as a medical secretary in London hospitals and in general practice, **Elizabeth Harrison** went to a voluntary medical organisation as associate editor. Here she was also responsible for arranging programmes in the UK for postgraduate doctors and nurses from overseas. She enjoys pottering about in boats, cooking in a slapdash way and trying to keep up with her garden overlooking Richmond Park. She is vice-president of the Romantic Novelists' Association.

Recent titles by the same author:

THE SENIOR PARTNER'S DAUGHTER
THE FAITHFUL TYPE
THE SURGEON SHE MARRIED
A SURGEON AT ST MARK'S

MADE FOR EACH OTHER

BY
ELIZABETH HARRISON

MILLS & BOON

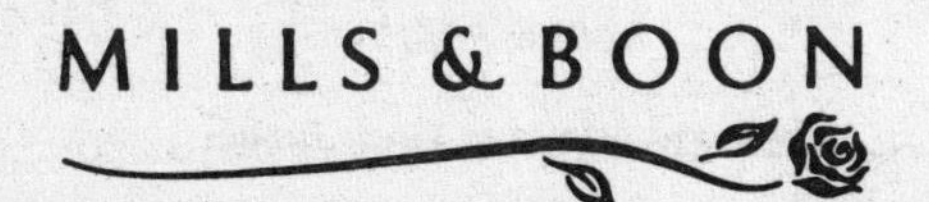

All the characters in this book have no existence outside the imagination of the author, and have no relation whatsoever to anyone bearing the same name or names. They are not even distantly inspired by any individual known or unknown to the author, and all the incidents are pure invention.

Harlequin Mills & Boon Limited,
Eton House, 18-24 Paradise Road, Richmond, Surrey TW9 1SR
This edition published by arrangement with Harlequin Enterprises B.V.

ISBN 0 263 79259 5

Set in Times 10½ on 11½ pt. by
Rowland Phototypesetting Limited
Bury St Edmunds, Suffolk

03-9508-46151

Made and printed in Great Britain

CHAPTER ONE

NORTHCLIFFE CHILDREN'S HOSPITAL, it had at last been decided, was to close, the children to be dispersed, some to their homes or to local authority care, others to the big general hospital, St Mark's, the other side of Halchester. They'd all seen this coming for months, yet it still shocked Kirsty. By autumn, the buildings would be empty and the site up for sale.

'Your job here is safe for the next six months, anyway,' Dr Field-Dalling told her. 'You'll be needed to handle the run-down and the final closure, and to ensure a smooth transition.'

Great. That would make a really jolly six months, she thought sourly.

She and Dr Field-Dalling were sitting together in her office after his weekly ward round. He'd stayed behind after the ritual tea and fudge-cake, dismissing the others, saying he had something to discuss with Sister Holt, if she could kindly spare him a few minutes.

'No problem,' she had answered automatically—and mistakenly, as it turned out. It became clearer with every word he uttered that there was going to be little else but problems ahead.

'However, the next six months is the least of it,' he went on. 'Always providing you are prepared to stay with us in Paediatrics—and speaking personally, I very much hope you are—there's a wide choice ahead of you.' He gave her his wide, endearing smile—grey-haired, small and spare, he had nevertheless always been a charmer, and now in his mid-sixties he remained one.

Kirsty found herself cheering up, as thousands of patients and staff had done before her. Perhaps the future was not that grim after all. At least it didn't sound as if she was going to be joining the dole queue yet.

'We shall continue to run children's Outpatients all over the county, so basically it'll be up to you what you do. There'll be a choice between a hospital post at St Mark's, the outpatient assignment, or alternatively you go on climbing the ladder and move to an administrative post. I wanted to get in first, have a talk to you about it while there's still plenty of time ahead. Now, as far as I'm concerned—and I'm not on the way out yet, I do still count for something in my own department, you know——' He beamed across the desk, and Kirsty, as expected, assured him fervently that his influence, as ever, was boundless and his youthfulness a phenomenon. 'Ah, well, just a year or two now,' he said. 'But you'll be around the department, if you want to be, years after I've gone.' He beamed again. 'They still miss you in Intensive Care, you know—they'd be delighted if you returned. But in my opinion you can do better than that. You'll have done nearly two years here, so you've administrative experience behind you now, as well as your nursing skills. Other doors are ready to open.'

Kirsty blinked the wide grey eyes that people told her were a knock-out, though she'd never believed them. What he said seemed incredible, but Dr

Fieldy, as the kids called him, never exaggerated. 'Such as?' she enquired dubiously, frowning, and pushing a straying blonde strand back into place.

'There's a new opening, an interesting one, which you might like to follow up. With child care centralised into St Mark's, we're planning a children's home-care service, a new link between hospital and home, flexible and adaptable, with instant admission to the wards for children on its books. Admission on demand, so to speak, so that parents know that, though they have their child at home with them, the hospital is wide open at any time of the day or night.'

'Sounds absolutely terrific,' Kirsty said, not allowing herself to dampen Fieldy's enthusiasm with the proviso 'if it works'.

'Well, it should be, provided we can make it work.'

She should have known. He was filled with common sense, always had his feet on the ground, even when his head was in the clouds.

'This home-care service,' he told her, 'will be run jointly by a consultant and a senior nursing officer. I'd like that nursing officer to be you.'

'Me?' Kirsty squawked inelegantly. She was taken aback. 'Me a senior nursing officer?'

'Obvious next step.'

He sounded almost impatient, she realised, amazed.

'Anything against it?'

'No. No, of course not. It'd be a wonderful opportunity. I—I'd love to be considered for it.' But she still couldn't quite believe in it.

'Good. That's settled, then. I've been planning this for years. Simply years, though frankly I never thought I'd be able to get it off the ground. Never any spare cash for innovations, the usual story, year after year. But now this place is to close, I've at last succeeded in getting it through, and I've always seen you as the ideal person to run it.'

'Oh, I do hope so,' Kirsty breathed ecstatically. This was a job to dream of, the sort of opportunity she'd never dared hope would come her way. And if Fieldy was right, it was practically going to be handed to her on a plate.

'How I see it is that we'll admit kids to the wards or Intensive Care for short periods only, with their mums whenever possible, teach their parents—fathers included, if we can—how to look after them, including their medication and as much of their treatment as they can take on board. We'll follow them up throughout with home visits and, as I said, admission on demand. An open-door policy. Everyone should benefit. With the short stays, we should have enough beds to cope with the local need, and small people with long-term illness can spend long periods—or even brief periods—at home instead of in hospital.' Suddenly his elderly features were young and filled with a powerful enthusiasm.

Kirsty was starry-eyed herself. 'It's an absolutely super plan. Do you really think you're going to be able to pull it off?'

'Touch wood, my dear, touch wood—we both know the health service too well to count on anything at all—but they've voted the budget, and I've clearance for both the consultant and your post.'

Her post. He was treating it as settled.

'I can't think of anything I'd rather do,' she told him honestly, her great grey eyes shining.

Fieldy twinkled at her. 'Thought that's how you'd feel,' he said smugly. 'It'll be a very varied job. You'll need to liaise with the district nurses and health visitors, remain in touch with Intensive Care and every advance or alteration in therapy, go into the homes yourself to check them out and help the mother if she's beginning to find it difficult to cope——'

'Yes, it'll be a strain for them. Stressing.'

'But they'll be in their own homes, doing the coping there. OK, it'll be stressful, but not necessarily more so than having a child in hospital and trying to cope in that strange environment. Of course, some of them won't be able to manage—selection, very careful selection, of both patients and parents, not to mention the home environment—will be vital. Selection will be a medical-nursing problem. Both paediatricians and nurses will have to work in the wards and in the home. You'll need staff nurses to go into the homes as well as yourself—but that's your problem. You'll handle the nursing admin, as well as the clinical side—you'll be the senior nursing officer, not the home-visiting sister.' He beamed.

'Never a dull moment.' Kirsty was radiant, her face alive with joyous anticipation, and her wide mouth curved into the heart-stopping smile for which she was famous in St Mark's—though of this she had not even the slightest suspicion. 'Thank you for thinking of me.' She smiled straight at him across the desk, and for a moment Fieldy, happily married for nearly forty years, longed to be young again and able to scoop her up for his own.

Instead, prosaically, he warned her she'd have

a difficult summer handling the run-down at Northcliffe. 'But you'll manage it well, I've no doubt of that, and it's going to be so worth while in the long run.'

Kirsty saw him to his car, and waved goodbye almost joyously. Whatever the difficulties, she'd cope. And it was all going to be, as Fieldy said, worth while.

In its day, Northcliffe Children's Hospital had been famous, with a long waiting list and a big permanent staff. Patients then had been children with bone and joint tuberculosis, rheumatic fever and its ensuing heart problems, and other conditions for which there had been no cure. Insulin, for instance, had not been discovered until the nineteen-twenties, and childhood diabetes was a killer.

After the Second World War, though, everything changed. Living conditions improved, tuberculosis at last became treatable with new drugs, and rheumatic fever, far from being common, more or less disappeared—although, astonishingly, Northcliffe harboured a child suffering from it at the moment.

Admitted to the acute ward in St Mark's from a caravan parked in a lay-by outside Halchester, Verity Blakelock was an underweight ten-year-old with a high fever and hot, painful, swollen joints. She was a very miserable child, distressed and with a racing pulse. The house physician from the children's ward, summoned to Casualty, had been foxed, and called the registrar, who had summoned Fieldy. He had diagnosed rheumatic fever instantly. When he'd been a medical student in London in the fifties, there had still been cases in the wards, and young women, too, with heart disease following rheumatic fever in childhood.

With treatment and careful nursing, Verity had improved immensely, but Fieldy had been adamant that she could not yet return to the steamy and poorly insulated caravan, which had been moved temporarily to one of the summer campsites.

'She needs complete bed rest until her temperature settles and her joints are free from pain. Let's get her to Northcliffe, where she can take her time and won't block an acute bed.'

She'd been with them for a month, but Fieldy said her temperature had not adequately stabilised, nor was he convinced the joint pain would not recur. What he was really afraid of, Kirsty saw, was sending her back to the wretched little caravan on the edge of a field above the cliffs. Verity was a lively, intelligent child, in spite of having had, as far as they were able to discover, almost no regular schooling—they'd moved around too much. Her mother was a charmer in sweeping skirts, colourful shawls, long dangling beads and a great deal of rather grubby beauty. She obviously loved her daughter, but seemed not to have the faintest notion how to look after her—indeed, Kirsty suspected it was Verity who did most of the looking after in that small family. But what was going to happen to her when Northcliffe closed she hardly dared to think. However, it was just one of the many problems she'd have to solve this coming summer, and no doubt she'd find a way.

Luckily, few of the children these days needed to stay for more than a week or two, and most of the parents were eager to have them back and keen to learn how to give them any treatment themselves whenever they could.

The exception was the school wing, now no longer part of the National Health Service, but run by an educational trust which leased the premises from St Mark's.

Northcliffe School, as it was called, accepted only asthmatic children, offering them a sheltered environment and schooling, so that here, as in earlier days, children stayed for years rather than weeks. The remaining wing now housed non-acute cases, post-operative or requiring medication too complicated for them to be looked after at home.

Kirsty had come to Northcliffe from St Mark's, where she had been in charge of paediatric intensive care. She'd moved to broaden her experience—hence, she reflected wryly, Fieldy's reference to ladder-climbing—though in fact that explanation had been more for public consumption than true. The real reason was that she had begun to find working in Intensive Care deeply depressing. They had lost too many children. It was, after all, the nature of the job. They took only dangerously ill and often hopeless cases, and those that did well left immediately for the ward, which meant that those who stayed longest and she had known best were the ones who died in spite of all their efforts. Losing a patient was always traumatic, but losing a child—or a tiny baby—was harrowing. Kirsty had known she could take no more of it, but she hadn't come clean about this. Recruitment to Intensive Care was never easy, and Kirsty had not wanted to be responsible for suggesting to nurses that they might hate it.

The demands on her at Northcliffe were quite different, and in some ways she'd found it a doddle, though perhaps only an intensive-care nurse could have found an eight- or ten-hour day among lively and obstreperous kids any sort of relaxation. But her depression had left her almost on arrival, and her job at the children's hospital had remained fun, as well as a challenge. Her time at Northcliffe had proved both enjoyable and illuminating. She'd had to adjust to an entirely different pace, much slower than in Intensive Care, and to give herself to the minutiae of running a small and understaffed hospital.

The staffing problem she'd solved brilliantly, everyone agreed. She'd seen what was needed, assessed what was available, and begun to make the rounds of all the local groups, which proved to be a rich source of volunteers. One of the previously untapped sources of help, to her surprise, had turned out to be the various pensioners' clubs. Elderly men and women were eager to be found capable of putting their energy and expertise into caring for sick youngsters, and soon she had had teams of them in the wards, reading to groups of children, playing games, walking inexpert youngsters on crutches, pushing the long carriages, left over from the days of tuberculosis of the bone, round the gardens, washing hands and faces, and, of course, helping at meals. It was hard work, and tiring, the volunteers agreed, but heart-warming, and they loved doing it.

When Kirsty had moved to Northcliffe, one of the imagined advantages had been that she would work regular hours, and days only. It had been a nice idea, but she had quickly found that attendance at local evening functions to drum up voluntary workers paid dividends. She'd never before done any public speaking, but she had soon learnt how to communicate effectively with increasingly large groups of individuals arrayed before her in rows. At first almost petrified with nerves, these days she found it stimulating and rewarding.

Now, though, the future was offering a different set of challenges. The coming six months of run-down might be a bit of a misery, with heart-break for children inevitable at first, a high anxiety level among their parents and the staff who were going to have to be redeployed—and what about her loyal volunteers? What was she going to do about them? Somehow she'd have to find a place for them in the new home-care scheme—though how, she certainly couldn't yet imagine.

She'd survive all the problems, though, she was confident of that, and then there'd be the new and unknown job, different from anything she'd taken on before.

She drove home happily, her eyes shining, her head buzzing with ideas and plans. Toby was coming for a meal, and she prayed he wouldn't be late—she could hardly wait to tell him her stupendous news.

Far too restless and excited to see to their meal at once, she raced upstairs to change out of uniform before she did anything else. Humming a happy little tune, she pulled on jeans and a sweater, and brushed out her fine blonde hair, not bothering to plait it or put it back into the knot she wore on duty. She was on a triumphant high. Oh, do hurry up, Toby. He'd be as thrilled as she was. Her career, her very own career, was going somewhere. She was even, she could say it without pushing it, beginning to be successful.

Suddenly she was ravenous. She looked at her watch. She shouldn't be—it was hardly late, and she'd had a slice of fudge-cake in the office with Fieldy. She must be burning up energy with sheer excitement, her metabolism racing.

The spiral staircase took her down to her open-plan living-room with the limed pine dresser dividing it from the kitchen, where the casserole she'd started off in the slow cooker before she left that morning smelt delicious—she'd put green and red peppers in it, as well as tomatoes. She'd thicken it up a bit now, and when Toby came she'd do baked potatoes in the microwave, and that would be it. Or maybe some carrots?

Good plan. She prepared them. They could go in the microwave after the potatoes—only take a couple of minutes. They could sit down to the meal as soon as Toby arrived.

She began setting her small round table, with its view across the garden towards the sea—while not large, her home was light and airy, with tall windows downstairs, while the attic bedroom upstairs had three dormer windows jutting out, through which the wind from the sea blew, salty and fresh.

She should have stopped on the way home to buy a bottle of wine to celebrate. A pity she hadn't thought of it. Too late now—she wasn't going to get the car out again.

She could ring Toby, though, try and catch him before he left, tell him to get one.

Too late. She heard his car outside.

She went to the door to meet him, and he came

racing across the drive, sturdy and ruddy, a bottle of wine in his hand, bursting with excitement. He must have heard already, on the grapevine, no doubt. Sweet of him to have thought of the wine.

'You've heard?' she said, hugging him.

'Isn't it great?' he said, hugging her back enthusiastically. 'Who'd have thought it possible? A new home-care service, with a new consultant post. Tailor-made for me. I'll be a consultant by the autumn, with any luck. I can buy a house and settle down. How about that?'

'Oh,' she said, on a dying fall, readjusting her ideas fast. The wine was for his new post, not hers. Well, after all, it could be for both of them, why not?

She went over to the kitchen counter, and started the potatoes. 'I actually have some news too,' she told him in a small careful voice. 'About the home-care service. Fieldy wants me to be the senior nursing officer running it.'

'Oh does he? Great. That'll be super, won't it? We'll be running it together—what could be more cosy?' He began opening the wine.

'Of course,' he said more soberly, 'it'll have to be advertised—but I should get it, wouldn't you say? After all, here I am on the spot, I'm Fieldy's senior registrar, I'm right in line. Wouldn't you say?'

What he said was absolutely true, but Kirsty had an uneasy feeling he was jumping the gun. True, he was Fieldy's senior registrar, but he hadn't held the post for as much as a year yet. He'd been his junior registrar before that, of course, and knew the department inside out. 'I certainly think you'd be bound to be in with a good chance,' she told him, 'especially if you have Fieldy's backing.'

'Bound to have that, wouldn't you think?' He was pouring the wine, and then tasting it, rolling it round his mouth. 'Mmm. Not bad, I'd say. See what you feel.' He brought her a glass.

She took it, raised it to him. 'To both our jobs,' she said. 'And to the home-care service. May we all be a sensational success.' She giggled briefly. 'The pride of St Mark's.' She took a mouthful of the deep red wine. 'Fantastic,' she said. 'Marvellous of you to have brought it.' Even if it was for you rather than for me, a small voice commented with a tinge of bitterness. 'It'll be perfect with the casserole,' she added hastily, irritated with herself for having niggly, censorious thoughts. Couldn't she just be pleased for both of them? Of course she could. She was.

'Smells wonderful,' he told her. Automatically, though, Kirsty saw. Lip service. He was really thinking about the consultant post. 'The new appointment starts on the first of October,' he said, bearing out her suspicions, 'so they'll have to advertise at once, if they're going to do interviews and give the successful candidate time to resign and have someone appointed to his post. That should be a new senior registrar at St Mark's, with any luck, don't you think?'

'Let's hope so,' she agreed. She hadn't the heart to dampen his ecstasy, but what did she really think? Was he in with a good chance, a reasonable chance, or an outside chance?

Impossible to say. A lot would depend on Fieldy, and he hadn't so much as mentioned the choice of the consultant when they'd been talking that afternoon. He'd talked only about the scheme itself, and her role in it. All the excitement she'd been feeling seemed to have ebbed, and now all she could think about was whether Toby was going to get the job or not, and whether he'd be completely thrown if he failed to land it. That was the problem with Toby. He lived on the heights or right down in the depths, never on the level ground between. She hoped, should he fail to be appointed consultant, he wouldn't take it too hard.

CHAPTER TWO

AT NORTHCLIFFE, all the doors had their handles set high up, so that small hands couldn't reach them, open them, and their owners speed away for parts unknown. The place was usually pandemonium, the noise level about as high as a disco, but more varied. All around, children were crying, exploding with laughter, or screeching at each other. Every ward was crowded for most of the morning and afternoon, not only with children and staff, but with hordes of others—parents, brothers, sisters, grannies, aunts, teachers, play leaders and Kirsty's regiment of volunteers—hardly any of them in uniform other than the cover-up pinnies donned by most of the staff.

There were seldom any acute cases there, but this merely added to the uproar and meant that the children were even noisier and more energetic. A walk through a ward demanded good eyesight and a high level of awareness, in order to dodge hurtling, chasing kids playing tig, speeding and erratically steered wheelchairs, abandoned toys, shoes, spoons, plates and bowls, dropped garments, or fragile items like spectacles or watches that had been grabbed and thrown as far as the thief could hurl them.

Survival required a cool head, an equable temperament and preferably a sense of humour too. Even so, exhaustion could easily set in long before the day was half over. Luckily Kirsty had always been resilient, but even so it was easy to reach what, without the long years of training behind her, would have been screaming point, and the coffee-break was always welcome. Then she could retire to her own office, by comparison a haven of peace and tranquillity, and settle down for a quiet chat.

This morning, she snatched the opportunity to bring her deputy, Emma Marston, up to date on what Fieldy had told her about the closure of the children's hospital and the inauguration of the new home-care service.

'So, come the autumn, we'll either be back in St Mark's or out of a job?' Emma, a dark and chubby foil to Kirsty's slender fairness, pursed her full lips in the way the male staff found such a come-on, or so Kirsty had been told, though she'd never been able to work out why.

'Fieldy seemed to think St Mark's would want us back,' Kirsty said. She didn't add to this, not chancing her arm. Whatever Fieldy had said, she wasn't going round boasting about her lovely new job until she actually had it in writing.

Emma had no doubts, though. 'You'll be running the new set-up, that's for sure,' she said comfortably. 'You've handled this place like a dream, Fieldy thinks the sun rises and sets over your head, and we all know Intensive Care have never really recovered from losing you. So they'll be competing for you at St Mark's, and you'll be able to take your pick, I shouldn't wonder.'

Kirsty blinked. Could this actually be true? 'Laying it on a bit thick, love,' she protested. 'No way am I flavour of the year at St Mark's. If you ask me, they've forgotten I exist since I'm out here in the backwoods.'

'You're certainly flavour of the year with Fieldy, and that's what counts. So I rely on you to find a niche for me in the new set-up. What about Toby? He must be aching to be the consultant—do you think he'll get the post?'

'I only wish I did—he's counting on it, I'm afraid, but I have an uneasy feeling that Fieldy may have someone much more senior in mind. Anyway, it'll have to be advertised, so who knows what may happen?'

'Won't it be absolutely super if he is appointed?' Emma was enthusiastic. 'The two of you running the new service between you? Imagine. Marvellous. Surely he's almost certain to get it? You'll be able to get married and settle down here in Halchester, instead of having to take off for unknown parts.'

'Honestly, Em, I've told you. Marrying Toby and settling down isn't part of my life's plan. I'm dreadfully fond of him, he's a great companion, but that doesn't mean I aim to spend the rest of my life with him. No way.'

'I do absolutely understand why you don't want to take anything for granted, but surely you can begin to relax at last and do a bit of forward planning? We all know Toby's been talking about looking at houses outside Halchester.'

Kirsty was well aware that, at both Northcliffe and St Mark's, wedding-bells were already pealing for her and Toby, and nothing she said ever changed their friends' conviction that she wasn't waiting nervily for Toby to land his consultant post so that they could buy this imaginary house and settle down to marital bliss. Though she protested and always denied plans for anything of the sort, they in their turn assumed her denials to be no more than a face-saving exercise, a refusal to admit she was hanging round waiting hopefully for any man. However, they never came out with this, merely murmuring agreeably, no, of course not, they were jumping to conclusions, sorry, forget it, while clearly going on believing exactly what they'd originally thought.

Kirsty gave up, not for the first time. 'Talking of forward planning,' she said, 'what we have to think about is what we're going to do about the kids and the volunteers, with closure ahead of us. That's going to be a real headache.'

'We're bound to lose most of our volunteers, aren't we? And they'll be truly upset about the place closing—a lot of them have been hoping and praying Northcliffe would somehow be saved at the last moment, and they'll be devastated.'

'I've been wondering if some of them can't be fitted into outpatient clinics near their homes, and maybe, if I can think out how to handle it, as they already know so many of the patients and their families, they'd help some of them in their own homes the way they do here. It would have to be managed through the home-care service, but if I can just work out a method of running a sort of voluntary home-help service——'

'That's a fabulous idea, if you can somehow pull it off. Because what most of them are dead scared of is St Mark's itself. A busy general hospital, not the free and easy outfit we have here—they think of it as stiff and starchy, very formal, flashing lights and bleeps going non-stop, and see themselves doing the wrong thing the instant they move, and being shouted at.'

Kirsty had to grin. 'Poor lambs, they should see the children's department, shouldn't they?'

'Oh, I dare say if we once got them there they'd have a change of heart, but I don't see how we'd so much as get them across the threshold. Even if St Mark's was likely to be in the least receptive to squads of untrained volunteers ready to work two hours every third day. You don't realise how miraculously you've run the volunteer system here.'

'No miracle. And I still want them, and if I can get the chance to say so, I jolly well will. But it is all going to take time, and the trouble is I could so easily lose them in the interim. And in any case, they're going to be upset and worried in the short term, and I don't see what we can do about that. Both of us must be fearfully upbeat and optimistic, and hope it's infectious, that's all.'

They both did what they could during the ensuing difficult months of closure, but it did turn out to be the volunteers who caused her the most headaches, rather than—to Kirsty's surprise—the children and their parents, who turned out to be far more flexible and forward-looking. Some of the children, indeed, seemed to look on the move to St Mark's as some kind of upgrading, like going on from junior school to the big comprehensive in the centre of town. Some of them, of course, were terrified of any change, but then, some kids in hospital were frightened most of the time anyway, and trying to reassure them part of a normal working day.

Another unexpected problem proved to be the

teaching staff, who got themselves into a lather because the school wing, with the long-stay asthmatic children, wanted to take over the whole building when the hospital closed, so that they could expand—they had a long waiting list for places. If this happened, most of the existing teachers in the hospital could transfer to the school, with no problems about moving house and family to another district. The problem was that the health service management could pull in more funds by selling the entire site, and all the buildings, to a property developer, and in this case, the school wing too would move to a new location. There were lobbies, and marches through the city centre, and a great deal of grief.

Meanwhile, Toby was in a state of exultant anticipation one day, certain he'd get the consultant post, and down in the depths of depression the next, as he was overtaken by an uneasy conviction that the opposition would be too much for him. When the post was advertised and the replies began to come in, he was thrown by the number of high-powered candidates.

'Half the candidates are consultants in post,' he moaned to Kirsty. 'As a senior reg, I may not even be in with a chance. What if they don't even short-list me?'

'Oh, I feel sure you'll be short-listed,' she said. What worried her was that it did begin to seem likely that this might be as far as he'd get. He was going to be so bitterly disappointed if he didn't succeed that her heart bled for him. His trouble was that he'd gone overboard at the start, counted too much on sailing through the board and taking over, and now he was finding it impossible to adapt to the possibility that he might not be appointed. She didn't like to be too cheerful and encouraging, to lead him on too much, as she was beginning to suspect that he had no more than an outside chance.

She was right about this. When the short list (of whom Toby was one) were interviewed, the post was offered to a consultant from a children's hospital in the north of England, Dr Grant Sheringham, Kirsty heard, who would take up his duties on the first of October.

She dreaded dealing with Toby that evening—and with reason. Irrationally, and in spite of his earlier forebodings and panics, he was furious. Consumed with rage and eager to blame the world rather than any shortcomings—or, more accurately, Kirsty knew, simple lack of seniority on his part—he held Fieldy responsible for his failure. If he wasn't going to back him, Toby repeated angrily and monotonously throughout the evening, Fieldy should never have allowed him to go ahead and put in for the job. He had encouraged Toby to believe he had his support.

Fieldy had let him down.

'I'm afraid he blames me,' Fieldy commented to Kirsty the next afternoon after his round. 'I do hope I didn't mislead him—I did try to get it across to him that he couldn't count on getting a consultant post the first time he applied. I was all for him putting in for it—good experience to go through these interviews. The fact that he's taking it so hard only demonstrates that, of course.'

'You know Toby,' Kirsty said. 'Right up or right down. No half-measures, no equilibrium. And he knew perfectly well at the outset that it was anything but a foregone conclusion.' She was a little snappish. Toby had taken it out on her all last evening, and then apparently on darling old Fieldy all this morning. 'Time he snapped out of it, though I'm afraid that towards the end he did get the whole thing right out of proportion, so I suppose it is going to take him a bit of time to get over his disappointment. I did try to warn him he shouldn't take it for granted.'

'I expected him to be disappointed, naturally, but it didn't occur to me he'd be totally thrown. I just hope it isn't going to mean that he'll find it in any way difficult to work with Dr Grant Sheringham.'

Oho. This was a warning, Kirsty saw, that she was meant to convey to Toby. And he'd better pull his socks up. Soonest. 'I expect,' she said with a confidence she in no way felt, 'he'll recover quite quickly, and get back to normal. He's not usually like this, after all,' she added, trying, she thought with a good deal of irritation, to excuse the inexcusable. How dared Toby take his disappointment out on Fieldy, of all people? And how daft of him, too. He needed Fieldy's backing for any future post, and it was plain silly to antagonise him, as well as unfair.

'We'll simply have to hope for the best.' Fieldy, now he'd delivered his cautionary message, dismissed the problem. 'Anyway, what I wanted to tell you was that next Friday I'll have Dr Sheringham with me on the round. He's coming down to stay with me next weekend, to see round generally, meet people, and discuss plans for the home-care service.'

'Oh, it'll be nice to meet him before he actually joins us in October,' Kirsty said.

'That's what I thought. You must come over some

time that weekend for a meal, and we can talk properly about the future.'

Suddenly Kirsty looked agonised. 'Oh,' she said on a gasp. 'Oh, thank you so much, but I'm afraid I can't. Not next weekend. It's—it's the christening of my sister's first baby, and I can't—I can't possibly miss it.'

'Of course you can't, my dear. An important family occasion, I'm sure. I wouldn't dream of suggesting you skip it—after all, you'll meet Grant Sheringham soon enough.'

Kirsty shook her head. 'I would really like to have met him before he actually joins us,' she said. 'And had a good talk with him about the new scheme.'

'Well, you'll meet him next Friday,' Fieldy pointed out. 'We must try and extend our talk then, that's all—or were you planning to get away early to go to your sister's?'

Kirsty had been, but she chose to deny it. 'No, no, I can easily go on Saturday—the christening isn't until Sunday. It won't matter at all.'

She was on edge still, Dr Field-Dalling could tell. Better encourage her to come clean about it. Unlike Kirsty to be so jumpy, but he'd gathered there was something unsatisfactory about her family background. Parents divorced, or something, family split up. 'Big family gathering?' he enquired.

Kirsty laughed shortly. 'That we shan't know until it's actually upon us,' she said sarcastically. 'Who'll arrive and who won't is in the lap of the gods.'

'You'll be your sister's main support, then?'

'Oh, my stepmother will be there all right. She won't let Julie down.'

'But the rest of the family will?' Fieldy probed.

He was fond of Kirsty, and he'd suspected more than once that something about her personal life was a struggle, though she'd never yet confided in him. Now he thought he might have hit on what it was, and he intended to make it easy for her to unburden herself. 'I suppose your father may find he can't get away,' he suggested. Almost the only fact he knew about Kirsty's background was that her father was the well-known heart surgeon Tom Holt, frequently featured on television screens climbing out of a plane or helicopter with a heart for transplant. A charismatic and brilliant surgeon, he might easily not be a noticeably devoted—or reliable—parent.

'Par for the course if he doesn't make it.' Kirsty's voice was bitter.

'So you think it may be just yourself and your stepmother?'

'Oh, my other stepmother may or may not turn up. That also won't be apparent until the hour itself. Perhaps I ought to explain,' she added. 'My own mother died when I was two. Since then my father has remarried twice, so I've two half-sisters and two stepmothers, and a more or less permanently absent father.' Her voice was hard as nails now, but her eyes were anguished.

Fieldy longed to be able to offer comfort, but knew there could be none for this pain. He said only, 'I do see it's absolutely imperative for you to be there. I'm so sorry you have these family problems to cope with.'

Kirsty shrugged. 'It happens. Can't pretend it's unusual, after all. We see it in our own kids' families all the time, don't we? Nothing in the least abnormal about it. Anyway, we're grown up now, and only one of us is living at home—it's all in the past. Finished with.'

'A broken family is always heart-break for someone,' Fieldy said sadly. 'And, as you say, we see it so often with our patients—in fact, we see it more than most, for there's not the slightest doubt that one damaged child is only too likely to damage the structure of the family in the long run.'

Kirsty sighed. 'Yes,' she agreed. 'First they face the strain of running the home and yet at the same time spending long hours, or often days and nights too, in what in itself is the stressing atmosphere of a busy hospital ward, all coupled with the anxiety they are experiencing for their child, and then, so often, they find the family crumbling beneath them.'

'It's impossible for any mother to get it one hundred per cent right,' Fieldy commented. 'They're either going to neglect the healthy kids and become over-protective of their sick child, or they manage to cope with both lots of kids at the price of neglecting their husbands. There, I have enormous respect for Jill Weybourne—and Kevin, too. Throughout Linda's treatment they've both been devoted and caring parents. They're still unmistakably united, and the other children seem to be doing fine, too.'

'Yes, the Weybourne family are true joy, aren't they?' Kirsty said at once. 'Whenever I feel down, or despairing about someone, I remember them, and I cheer up. I'm so glad we've succeeded in installing Linda at home, respirator and all.'

Fieldy smiled back at her. 'One of our undoubted successes,' he said, and touched wood hastily. 'I shouldn't be superstitious,' he added, 'but I am.'

Linda Weybourne was the eldest of Kevin and Jill's three daughters. At ten years old, she had dived unsuspectingly off a bridge into a shallow river, and broken her neck. Now, at thirteen, she was paralysed. Her parents had visited her and taken it in turns to stay with her at the spinal injuries centre in Stoke Mandeville for over a year, and then she had been transferred to St Mark's, to be nearer her family.

Soon after Kirsty's own move to Northcliffe, Linda had been moved there, too. She was not ill, but she needed twenty-four hour care, though a casual observer might not have suspected this. She had a powered wheelchair specially adapted for her, so that her back and neck were supported, and her wrists cradled in an arm-rest—she had slight movement in fingers and thumb on her right hand, and in the tips of two fingers on the left. Electronic gadgetry meant that she was able to make use of this to steer her chair, and to feed herself or turn the pages of a book if it was placed in a rack for her. Her spirit was indomitable, she was fun to be with, had a huge sense of humour, and, as far as could be seen, her entire family adored her.

Recently, among the changes that were taking place during the closing down of Northcliffe, Linda had gone to live with her family. There had been alterations to the Weybournes' house by the council and, among these, an extra bathroom had been installed, with lifts and pulleys. Then, too, a vast team of assistants had been assembled to care for her, professionals and volunteers working together.

Both Fieldy and Kirsty were secretly proud that

they had managed to achieve this new life for Linda, which they had frequently doubted they were going to be able to pull off. The obstacles, in fact, had been formidable—but now Linda was home, and, better still, the system was working.

Fieldy reverted to more pressing problems, they settled their outstanding queries, and then he departed. 'Don't forget I'll be bringing Grant Sheringham next week,' he reminded her.

As if she could.

'The round's bound to take longer than usual, I'm afraid, what with introducing him to everyone and going into past histories, as well as discussing patients we're still planning to move.' He gestured at one of the papers littering Kirsty's desk. 'That lot—you'll try and get parents here for me, if at all possible, won't you?'

'I'll do my best,' she promised.

'Sorry you're not going to be able to join us for a meal at the weekend—I'm planning to take Grant and Toby to Long Barn for lunch, and I'd hoped you'd be with us. Can't be helped, though—have a good christening, in case I don't get a chance to mention it next week. I do hope most of them turn up.'

'Me, too,' Kirsty told him.

But her eyes now were unworried, he saw, and he decided with relief that her family problems were in the past. She had a full and absorbing life here in Halchester, with young Toby to support her.

Kirsty was thinking about Toby, too. They were meeting for the evening meal, which he'd offered to provide—this almost certainly meant an Indian take-away in his flat, but it would be an opportunity to talk without flapping ears around. She'd be able to tell him about Grant Sheringham next week, and let him know Fieldy was planning to take him to lunch with Grant.

His reaction was grumpy. 'Long Barn?' he repeated. 'Trying to soften me up, is he?'

Kirsty was exasperated with him. 'I only wish someone would think of trying to soften me up with lunch at Long Barn,' she said crisply.

Much frequented by St Mark's consultants, Long Barn was the most renowned restaurant for miles. Meals there cost an arm and a leg, however, and junior staff went there only for outstandingly important celebrations.

'Anyway,' she added, 'that's the weekend. On Friday they're both coming over to Northcliffe for the round, and afterwards we're to have a good talk about the community care service. So by the end of next week we'll both know a good deal more about Grant Sheringham.'

'Oh, I know what he's like,' Toby told her unexpectedly. 'He came down to look us over as soon as he was short-listed, wouldn't you know? Fieldy brought him round then. It was on a Saturday, and they both walked into the ward together without any warning. I'd been trying to get away early, too.'

'You never told me you'd met him.' Kirsty was indignant.

'You never asked. And we didn't know then that he was actually going to be appointed, either. Several of the short list looked in at one time or another. He was the only one who stayed over the weekend, though. Sucking up to Fieldy, that's what, if you ask me. It was my Sunday off, but the theatre said they had him there with Fieldy for an emergency on Sunday morning, then they had lunch at Fieldy's, and then they both went to Northcliffe in the afternoon. Of course you would have been off, so you wouldn't have seen him.'

'Never mind the timetable. Just tell me what he's like.'

'Tall, dark and handsome,' Toby said derisively. 'Taller than me. One of those big-shouldered, massive blokes, more like an orthopod than a paediatrician. Bovine, I'd say.'

Well, of course, he had to say something derogatory, Kirsty could see that, especially if Grant Sheringham was taller than he was, something Toby never endured easily. Mentally she deleted bovine from Grant Sheringham's characteristics—in any case, Fieldy would hardly have supported a bovine hunk for the post.

'Slow-moving,' Toby was continuing. 'Slow-spoken. Phlegmatic.'

Well, he'd need to be phlegmatic to deal with Toby in this mood, wouldn't he? Kirsty kept this reaction to herself. 'Roll on next Friday,' she said. 'All will be revealed.'

Toby had been bang on about one point, Kirsty realised the moment Fieldy and Grant Sheringham stepped into the hall at Northcliffe punctually at two o'clock the following Friday. He was massive. A huge man, he towered over Fieldy and herself. He also managed, though she hadn't the slightest idea how, to radiate calm and quiet confidence. Perhaps that was what Toby had meant by bovine. And he was, no doubt about it, extremely handsome. The enormous shoulders were topped by a head with rugged features, dark eyes—dark, penetrating eyes, with dark bushy brows above, jutting, and crisp dark hair above that, cut fairly short and clearly trying its best to curl at the nape of the neck, an endearing feature, that, and Kirsty was startled to discover herself longing to put out a hand and touch those infant curls.

She must be out of her tiny mind. Furious with herself, she responded more formally than she would normally have done to Fieldy's introduction, and Grant Sheringham—since he was in fact neither bovine nor phlegmatic—picked up the cool reserve at once, and guessed the reason. She resented him because he had taken the post her future husband had wanted. Fieldy had explained carefully that Toby Gresham, the senior registrar in Paediatrics, had put in for the consultant's post, and been short-listed for it, too. He'd been bitterly disappointed not to get it, and Grant might find him a slight problem to handle at first, while he was still on edge about not getting the job.

'But he's a sensible chap. He'll come round quickly, I'm sure, return to his normal co-operative self.' He prayed he was right about this. 'Just at first, though, there may be a little awkwardness, perhaps some stiffness on his part.' He shrugged. 'Well, these things happen. Pay no attention.'

But Grant had met other St Mark's consultants over drinks at the Field-Dallings', and they'd fore-cast that he'd encounter trouble with Toby Gresham, adding, too, that the newly appointed senior nursing officer running the home-care service,

Kirsty Holt—lovely girl—was Toby's intended. In fact, everyone knew that if Toby had been appointed to the consultant post, they'd planned to marry and buy a house locally. Whether that was now off or not remained to be seen, but they'd hardly be buying a house when Toby might have to go anywhere in the country for a consultancy. Toby Gresham had always maintained, he heard, that there was no question of marriage for him before he had a consultant post.

So this stiff and formal lady was presumably blaming him not only for having snatched the senior job away from her beloved, but also for doing her out of marriage and retirement to a dream house to raise a family.

Hard cheese. She'd have to come to terms with it. And to the fact that he was the consultant, too.

Not, in all fairness, that there was anything in her manner that he could put his finger on. He had no real grounds for complaint—her behaviour was impeccable. In fact, that was what was wrong with it. It was inhuman, and certainly the reverse of friendly. She might have had a poker down her back, her eyes were cool and assessing, her tone frigid. Blonde and undoubtedly beautiful, she was the ice-maiden in person.

Ah, well, new jobs always brought new problems. Clearly she was going to be one of them. But he'd weather them both, this disapproving nursing officer and the displaced Toby Gresham. With whom, he reminded himself, he had to have lunch tomorrow. So he'd put the problem of Ms Kirsty Holt on one side, forget about her. He could begin to grapple with her arctic personality when he was actually in post next month. Tomorrow was Toby Gresham, and he needed to find out how to deal with him pretty smartly.

It was a pity, though, he felt, as he and Fieldy drove away together after a fascinating round, a mass of introductions that he'd somehow sort out later, and a stiff little tea party with senior staff in the office. Kirsty Holt was a lovely girl, and in other circumstances he'd be planning to date her fast. And often. Those eyes—he saw them still in his mind. Unforgettable.

But apart from her strange personality, she was off limits. Booked. She was going to marry Toby Gresham. No way could he sweep in and snatch his blonde as well as his job.

Though the prospect was enticing. To break down that glacial reserve, bring life into those great grey eyes—no, he mustn't even think of it. Off bounds.

CHAPTER THREE

KIRSTY and Emma were just leaving the smart new office in what had originally been the empty ward at the top of the children's wing at St Mark's, but was now the home of the Children's Community Care Service. They were on their way to the inaugural meeting, when the telephone rang. Her chic new secretary would deal with it, Kirsty thought thankfully. Even so, she paused in the doorway, just in case.

Rightly, it seemed. Ominously, her secretary was saying, 'Hold on a moment—I'll see if I can catch her. She's on her way to a meeting, but I'll try to call her back for you.' Hand over the mouthpiece, 'Your sister Julie,' she told Kirsty. 'Says it's a bit urgent.'

'OK, I'll take it. You go on ahead, Em, and I'll follow as soon as I can. Explain I got held up, if you need to, but I'll try not to be long.'

Julie. And if she was saying it was urgent, that was what it was. Of all moments for a piece of family drama, this was about the worst. But Julie never rang her at work unless there was some sort of crisis.

'I'm terribly sorry, love, to ring you at the hospital,' Julie said hurriedly, 'but I had to warn you.'

Warn her? She knew it. 'What about?'

'Fran seems to be on her way to join you.'

'Oh, *no*. Today of all days. That's all I need.'

'Well, I'm afraid she's liable to turn up on your

doorstep tonight or tomorrow, and, as ever, she'll expect you to drop everything and minister. Apparently she got bored staying with Mum, too quiet and no night-life——'

'Halchester's night-life is not exactly riveting, and she's normally bored out of her mind inside two days when she stays with me,' Kirsty pointed out. She'd often wished it wasn't so. 'There's nothing interesting to do, she complains always.'

'Well, natch, she'd rather be somewhere more exciting—she said so—but according to her, there's nowhere else for her to go. Annabel's in the States, and won't come up with the air fare, apparently.'

'There's always Harley Street. More exciting than Halchester any day. Much more going on. And I bet she could wheedle the air fare out of Dad, if she gave her mind to it.'

'She seems to want to keep out of his way.'

'Oh, lord, she's gone and done something she knows he'll disapprove of, so she's running scared and trying to avoid him until it's blown over, as ever.'

'That's right. So she's escaping to you, and you'd better be ready for it. Now, listen, don't let her walk all over you the way you usually do, and don't wait on her hand and foot, either.'

'I'll do my best,' Kirsty said lightly, though she knew what Julie meant, and suspected it might be only too true. She was inclined to be weak with Fran.

'That's all I wanted to say. I'll get off the line and you can get back to whatever you're in the middle of. But remember, don't turn into a doormat. Right. Over and out.'

'Hang on, pet. How is our lovely baby?'

'Thriving. Me too. No problems for you there, at least. I'll be in touch.'

Kirsty put the telephone down, and firmly, with the habitual expertise of years, pushed Julie, the new baby, and the imminent arrival of Fran into the furthest recesses of her mind. 'Thanks for trying, anyway,' she said to her secretary. 'I'm off again. Second time lucky, maybe.' She stepped out of the office, to outward appearance as cool and unflurried as ever, head high, her blonde hair folded smoothly into its knot at the nape of her elegant neck, her dark blue uniform fitting like a glove and swaying fascinatingly as she moved. This in fact was not the outfit she intended to wear on duty with the home-care service, but for today's meeting it would do no harm to appear crisp and professional, even if, visiting children and parents in their homes, she preferred to look informal and approachable. Her shoes clicked fast along the corridors until, with barely a second to spare, she slid silently into the only empty seat on the platform—next to Fieldy himself, she found, who was in the chair, with Grant Sheringham on his other side. In a funny sort of way, Kirsty had to accept it, she too was now part of the hierarchy. It felt odd. Incredible, actually. But the new service was to be run jointly by Grant Sheringham, its director, and herself, its senior nursing officer. She could, she supposed, be said to have arrived.

Today she seemed to have moved up another notch, she discovered. Fieldy was standing up to start the meeting, welcoming everyone and giving them a spiel about the new service. Its medical director, he explained, was Dr Grant Sheringham, on his right, and its nursing director Miss Kirsty Holt, on his left.

People clapped, and Kirsty, to her inner fury, blushed a brilliant scarlet. Just in time, she remembered she mustn't scowl, and tried instead to smile serenely at the serried ranks of GPs, health visitors, district nurses, social workers, physiotherapists, plus the entire staff of St Mark's children's department.

Unexpectedly, Fieldy was now handing the chair over to Grant Sheringham, and taking himself off, pausing to shake hands meticulously not only with Grant, but with Kirsty, before departing.

Grant moved into the chair next to her—or, at least, to the space in front of it, as he stayed on his feet, and took over control of the meeting, his broad-shouldered, bulky figure towering over her in its dark, expensive consultant's suiting. After a few brief formal sentences about his pleasure in his appointment to St Mark's and its new unit, his thanks to Dr Field-Dalling for his support, not to mention his assistance in planning the new set-up, the value of his unparalleled experience over the years in the care of children from Halchester and the local countryside, he moved on to talking about the future.

'Before I go into detail about our plans for running the new system, which I and our nursing director will be running jointly, I want to say a few words about Miss Holt. I am fortunate indeed to be able to call upon her experience both in St Mark's and in Northcliffe, and I know that you will all agree with me when I say that we are immensely lucky to have her.'

More applause. Kirsty was shattered. She'd never supposed he'd felt anything of the sort, let alone come out with it on a public platform like this.

He was still talking about her, laying it on thick, she considered, though this time round she managed not to blush in that silly childish way. Instead she sat imperturbably at his side, looking, she trusted, pleasantly receptive though not, of course, in the least smug, but totally unaware that her huge grey eyes were shining brilliantly. When he finally ended she was in complete control of herself, and rose confidently to her feet, giving him her infectious smile, and going ahead in her best platform style—all those evening meetings drumming up volunteers and financial support for Northcliffe had honed and polished her speech-making to a fine art—to say how equally lucky they were to have Dr Grant Sheringham, how much they were going to enjoy working together as a team, and how challenging and invigorating it was for all of them to be in at the start of this new and enormously promising development in paediatrics—one day, she was certain, to be a blueprint for child care nationwide.

Grant Sheringham was transfixed. All right, so Fieldy had kept on telling him Kirsty Holt was a treasure, unflappable, resourceful, superbly capable, but Grant had had his doubts, and he'd certainly never imagined she'd attain this level of mastery in handling a meeting. She must have unsuspected depths, and Fieldy had been spot-on when he'd maintained that the rigid formality she'd displayed on that first stiff round at Northcliffe was absolutely untypical. Evidently she'd recovered from her irritation with him for snatching the post away from Toby Gresham, and so he was seeing a different side of her personality. About time, too. But it did actually look as if he might even begin to enjoy working with her. A pity she was permanently partnered by Toby Gresham, though. What a waste of such a lovely creature. What idiots women could be, throwing themselves away on hopeless cases. No. He was being unfair. Toby was not any sort of hopeless case—no need to exaggerate. All it was, Grant reminded himself firmly, was that he had been pipped at the post, he hadn't got over it yet, and so he was being difficult. But he wasn't nearly good enough for Kirsty Holt, that was for sure. She was, exactly as Fieldy had told him, quite simply a treasure. Here she sat coolly at his side, dealing with tricky questions from the floor with absolute poise and consummate skill—humour, too, where it helped—chipping in to support him at fraught moments, and generally being a tower of strength. Already, in this, their first assignment together, they were a team.

He was enjoying himself. He'd looked forward with such high hopes to this post, his opportunity to launch a new and untried system for continuing care in the community with open admission to the wards, and here it was all under way at last, and going well, too.

As the meeting finally broke up, he turned happily to Kirsty and asked if she'd join him for a meal. They could tie up any loose ends, and lay a few plans for the week ahead. 'Though I promise not to talk shop throughout,' he added hastily, as her face clouded. What it must be, of course, he should have realised, was that she was already booked to eat with blasted Toby. He'd been mad to suppose she might be free.

'I would have loved to,' she was saying, with what sounded like genuine regret, 'but I'm afraid I'm already committed.'

Exactly as he'd feared.

'The thing is,' she went on, 'I've invited most of the staff back to my place for a meal.' Uncertain how to proceed, she hesitated. She could go ahead and invite him to join them, but would he want to be involved in what amounted to a duty evening, that was in no way going to be *haute cuisine*, either? Mentally she shrugged. She could but ask him; he only had to say no. 'Would you like to join us? You'd be very welcome, but I'm afraid it'll be a bit of a scramble—simply pizza delivery. I'm going to ring the final number through now, before I leave. They're supposed to be standing by to zoom out with it as soon as I give the word. Could you stand pizza and salad with more or less the entire staff?'

'Nothing I'd like better,' he said immediately, and smiled at her in a way that suddenly made him look years younger—almost boyish, in fact, as his dark eyes looked straight into hers.

She took a quick breath, almost a gasp. What was happening? She was merely fixing a routine meal for the staff, which now seemed to include the new director, but so what? Nothing to it, and certainly not the faintest excuse for feeling as if she had taken off wildly into a state of brilliant promise and surging excitement.

She must pull herself together. Ring up the pizza firm. Behave like a sane human being, arranging a busy departmental evening. Making a tremendous effort, she stiffened her spine, unconsciously giving Grant a distinctly stony glare for good measure.

He was still talking. 'It's just what we need after the meeting,' he told her. 'Splendid of you to have seen to it—I'm afraid I'm still at rather a disadvantage there. I don't yet know people well enough to have laid anything on for them myself. Tell me how to get to your place, and I'm on my way,' he ended cheerfully, though he was asking himself what on earth he'd done now, to make her throw him this unmistakably frosty stare, quite out of the blue. However, luckily he had his mind with him in spite of Kirsty's unsettling glances. 'Or can I give anyone a lift?' he added.

'If you would, that would be a help. We're meeting in the car park, and I was planning to pack them all into whatever cars are available.'

'Right. Count me in. Perhaps I could take someone who already knows the way?'

'Good plan. Tell you what, you take Emma and go on ahead with her. Her own car is having its MOT, but she helped me with the advance preparations last night, so I'll give her my keys and she can open up and be ready for the delivery, while I stay here, ring up the pizza people, and get everyone sorted out and into the cars. Would that be all right?'

'Fine. I'll go and get hold of Emma, and we'll be on our way.'

Kirsty handed him her house keys, he went in search of Emma, told her what they were to do, and they set off.

'Kirsty lives in what used to be the stables, at the back of one of those big Victorian houses up on the cliffs,' Emma said. 'It's quite small, but spacious—

one big room downstairs, with an open-plan kitchen, a spiral staircase, which I love, up to a big sort of loft room with dormer windows looking out to sea. Terrific views.'

'Sounds interesting,' Grant said. This was the exact truth. Did she, or did she not, live there with Toby? was what interested him.

'It can absorb a huge number of people when necessary, and Kirsty can always help herself to trestle-tables and folding chairs from what was the coach-house next door, which the owners of the main house use for parties and dances themselves, and also lend to local good causes for bazaars and jumble sales, and so on.'

Somehow it didn't really sound as if Kirsty and Toby were actually living together, Grant decided, and then stopped short. What the heck did it matter to him, in any case? Mind your own business, Grant Sheringham, and keep out of Kirsty Holt's private life. You and she have been appointed to run the Children's Community Care Service, not to embark on a relationship. Any emotional involvement between them could jeopardise the service in its early days, not to mention antagonise Toby Gresham even more. Hands off Kirsty Holt, keep any contacts strictly professional. Had she herself sensed that they could run a dangerous risk there? Was that what lay behind that unexpected icy glare just now?

'It's this next drive, on the right, Highcliffe,' Emma said. 'You go on past the house, right down to the end, and this is it, here.'

'Charming,' he said. And it was. Built of the same red brick as the turreted mansion they'd passed, the stables, originally only one storey high with a loft above, benefited from the simpler lines of Victorian purpose-building as opposed to the status and grandeur displayed in the design of the main house. The conversion, too, into a small dwelling, had been carried out with imagination. There were full-length windows at either side of the front door, and three dormers in the steeply sloping tiled roof above. When Emma unlocked the door and led the way inside, Grant realised that the interior was flooded with light. It was also fairly crowded with what he realised must be the trestle-tables Emma had mentioned, covered now in striped pink and white cloths.

'We did those last night so as to be ready,' Emma explained. 'Kirsty thought people could collect their own chairs from the coach-house, which I have to unlock—don't let me forget. But I'll take you upstairs and show you the rest of the house first.' She began to ascend the graceful spiral with its white curving banisters. On the next floor the roof sloped, and the three dormer windows looked much larger than they had done from outside, flooding this room, too, with a strong light from the sea. There were two divans, one at either end of the long room, built-in cupboards right along the wall opposite the windows, a blanket chest used as a dressing-table between two windows, a chest of drawers in the other gap, a couple of rush-seated, slatted-back armchairs in pine, and a door at the end of the room leading to the bathroom, Emma said. 'There's no cloakroom downstairs, so people will have to come up here, and Kirsty thought they could dump their belongings here too, as it's going to get more than a bit crowded downstairs by the time everyone's in.

Nice, isn't it? I always envy her.'

'It's delightful. And the views of the sea and the cliffs are quite spectacular.' He was staring out of one of the dormer windows, which were curtained with the same pink-striped cotton that covered the tables downstairs.

'I like the colours, don't you?' Emma was enthusing. 'The stripped wood everywhere, and the rush matting—it all adds up to a fantastic look, I think. Apparently the people in the big house went a bit overboard when they converted this place for their only daughter. Interior by Smallbone, no less.'

'Are they pricey?' The name meant nothing to Grant. 'I'm afraid I'm not exactly up in interior decoration—I just know what I like, and I certainly go for this.'

'Smallbone cost the earth, and then some. They do fitted kitchens and bedrooms, in lovely woods and with superb craftsmanship. I gather what happened was that they did the huge Victorian kitchen in the main house, and the family were so impressed they splurged out and got them to do the kitchen here, and then the fitted cupboards. It's all in this pale limed pine, which I do think looks super. And after all that, the daughter went and married before she'd lived in it for as much as a year, and so they let it out to summer visitors—I think they were relieved to have a year-round tenant like Kirsty. Help, I shouldn't be standing around chatting like this. I must go and open the coach-house before they all start arriving.' She turned and clattered down the spiral staircase.

Grant followed more slowly. Kirsty's home was enchanting, he decided, and for a brief, mad moment he imagined her moving around it, accompanied not by Toby but by himself.

Gravel crunched outside. The pizza delivery had begun, and in no time the little cottage was buzzing with talk and seething with activity. Half the children's department poured in, some in uniform, others in their party-going gear, others in jeans. Emma unpacked pizzas and salads and set them out on the trestle-tables, while Grant established a mini-bar on the counter top between the kitchen and the living-room. There were bottles of Coke and Diet-Coke, supplied by Pizza Express, Perrier from Kirsty's fridge, bottles of white wine, and orange juice, Emma told him. 'There should be some red wine out on the counter somewhere, I think you'll find. Kirsty thought an awful lot of people will probably stick to Coke, though, as they'll be driving, and a good many of them going back on duty. The glasses, I'm afraid, are still in the coach-house. I'll go across with a tray and start shifting them in a minute.'

'Not to worry. I'll go across for them.'

'Oh, but——' Emma was sure Kirsty would disapprove of the new consultant being put into service as barman and waiter, and she began assuring him he'd already done more than enough—why not just pour himself a drink and take a seat?

'No problem,' he told her. 'Plenty of time for sitting down and knocking it back later on. I'm on my way.' He seized a tray, and was out of the door before she could stop him.

In any case, the telephone rang. Emma picked it up, and gave Kirsty's number.

She was answered by a young and frantic voice.

'Kirsty?' it enquired. 'That's not you,' it added. 'Oh, I haven't got the wrong number, have I? I can't bear it. I've no more change—no more money at all, for that matter. Who *is* that?'

Emma had already guessed who was on the line, and she was inwardly cursing. This was all Kirsty needed on this hectic evening at the end of an exhausting week, her spoilt youngest sister. That would have been what the earlier call had been about, of course. 'This is Emma,' she announced in her most ward-sister, stand-no-nonsense voice. 'Is that Fran?'

'Oh, how terribly clever of you, Em. I would have thought you'd have forgotten my existence by now. You *are* a sweetie. Look, is Kirsty there? Because I'm here at the station, and I'm absolutely counting on her to come and fetch me and my luggage.'

'No way.' Emma wasn't going to stand for this. 'Kirsty has almost the whole department here to feed. You must get a taxi, Fran.'

'Oh, but Em, angel, I haven't got any cash for a taxi, I'm down to my very last pennies, truly. If Kirsty's all tied up with mobs of people, couldn't you collect me instead? It wouldn't take long, now, would it?'

She was wheedling like the child she fundamentally remained, although surely she must be in her twenties by now? Emma was thankful Kirsty hadn't yet put in an appearance, since if she had been there she'd very likely have dropped everything and gone tearing off to Halchester station for this spoilt chit, never mind what was going on here. 'It would take me at least half an hour to come and fetch you,' she said repressively. 'And anyway, my car's having its MOT, so I haven't got any transport to fetch you or anyone else.'

'Oh, but couldn't you use Kirsty's car? Do, please, Em.'

'Just get a taxi, Fran, it's much the easiest way—and the quickest, too. One of us will pay the fare when you arrive.'

'Please, Em, surely you can find someone from all those people to come in and fetch me?'

'They're still arriving, Fran, we've had this big meeting. Everyone's tired and hungry, and I'm not grabbing hold of anyone and telling them to get back into their car, turn round and drive back to the other side of Halchester, when you can perfectly well hop into the nearest taxi.' Dealing with Fran was sheer hard work, and Emma began to see why Kirsty so often took the line of least resistance 'When you get here, we'll pay the fare, so there's no problem. Get a taxi, and you can have pizza and wine as soon as you arrive. See you then.' She put the telephone down before Fran had a chance to protest again, and returned to the tables.

Within a minute or two, Kirsty herself appeared.

'Your young sister rang,' Emma informed her. 'She was at the station, and she wanted you to fetch her. So I told her no way, she must get a taxi—she said she had no money, so I promised we'd pay the fare when she got here.'

'Oh, blow. Isn't that just what would happen? Julie did ring to say Fran was on her way, but I was hoping maybe it wouldn't be until tomorrow—I thought she'd go back to Harley Street first. Thanks for taking the call and sorting her out, anyway.'

'Glad to,' Emma said airily, not letting on that she'd fought a mini-battle. 'That's everything out on the tables, so we can go ahead and eat.'

'Great. Thanks again, Em, for seeing to everything like this. Come on, everyone, you can sit down and eat. It's all on the tables—get stuck in.'

They were just about settled, all of them had pizza and a drink, though the salad was still going round and chunks of French bread being passed, when Fran erupted through the door and into the room.

More beautiful than Emma had remembered, she succeeded in causing a mild sensation, as she no doubt intended, Emma decided grumpily. Wearing pale flowery leggings with a brilliant tangerine shirt beneath a wide fluffy mohair scarf, her blonde hair permed and framing her features in feathery curls, she opened her arms as if to embrace them all, shrieking, 'Kirsty darling, it's been far too long, oh, isn't it simply super to see you? Sweetie, can you pay the taxi? I haven't a single penny.'

A sudden silence had fallen over the room, and the final phrase emerged like a solitary clarion call.

Magically, how she couldn't imagine, Grant had materialised at Kirsty's side.

'I'll see to it,' he said, and was out of the front door before she could begin to stop him.

Conversation resumed, though sporadically, while eyes stayed glued to the two sisters. They made a striking pair. Half a head taller than Kirsty, Fran was a dramatic contrast, with her cascade of blonde curls and her vivid, leggy look, to the fine-drawn Kirsty, still in nursing officer's crisp navy, her hair pinned up close to her head as she wore it on duty.

Grant reappeared, carrying a vast and bulging

case, a tote-bag slung across one shoulder, a canvas hold-all in his free hand. 'All seen to,' he announced shortly. 'I'll take this lot straight upstairs, right?' Ignoring Kirsty's protestations, he strode across the room, navigating miraculously around tables and chairs, his long legs fast disappearing upwards, as though the weight he carried was negligible.

Kirsty's were not the only eyes that followed him, either. More than half the room watched, and not least Fran.

'Oh, gosh,' she sighed. 'I think it may be much more exciting staying with you than I'd expected.'

Kirsty had to smile. Typical Fran. 'That might have been more tactfully put,' she murmured. 'And there was I imagining you loved me for myself alone.'

'Oh, sweetie, you know I do really. It's just, well, I mean, you must see——'

'Oh, I do. Believe me, I do.'

Toby joined them, a slice of pizza in his hand. 'You never said Fran was arriving tonight,' he rebuked Kirsty. 'If I'd realised, I could have picked her up at the station on my way out here.'

He seemed genuinely put out, Kirsty saw. 'Yes, well, if she'd let me know in time, we could have arranged it, couldn't we?'

'Oh, but, honeybunch, don't say you had no idea?' Fran exclaimed in dismay. 'How perfectly awful—I made sure Julie would be bound to ring you.'

'Oh, she did. But it was only just before the meeting, and anyway, I didn't expect you until tomorrow—I thought you'd go to Harley Street tonight.'

'Well, yes, I did plan to, but then I decided, why bother? I changed at the junction, and although I had to get a slow train, stopping every few minutes at the most weird little places, I must say—which is why I'm so fearfully late, not to mention absolutely ravenous—it seemed much simpler to come straight to you. So here I am.' She smiled meltingly. 'You don't actually mind, do you, sweetie?' She smiled again, but it was a much younger smile, more of a teenager's grin. 'And I'm just in time for this super binge—can I have some of that delish pizza?'

'Of course you can. This minute. Come along, and I'll feed you.' Toby took her arm at once, and guided her possessively across the room to his own seat, into which he settled her as if she were a piece of delicate porcelain, about to shatter without the most tender handling.

Kirsty felt like braining him. The deluded idiot couldn't resist competing with Grant, even over someone like Fran, whom he'd met often, and previously almost ignored. She hadn't missed his quick glance over to the stairs before he'd grabbed Fran and led her off.

She walked across and met Grant as he returned. 'That was so very kind of you,' she told him. 'I'm so grateful. How much do I owe you for the taxi?'

'Forget it for now. Pay me next week.' He was dismissive, and then he grinned, and she knew everything was all right—would go on being all right, too. Forever. Or something. 'Don't worry,' he went on. 'I'll remind you, I promise. But no point in fiddling about now sorting out our loose change. Time you sat down yourself and took in some nourishment—I've kept us both chairs over there, and I got you some food, too, so come along and eat it.' In his turn, he took Kirsty solicitously by the arm, across the room, and sat her down in front of a huge—and delightful, since she was starved—plateful of assorted slices of pizza, mixed salads and chunks of garlic bread. There was a glass of her Bulgarian red, too, and by now she felt she needed it.

'You're one person who's not going to be driving anywhere tonight, and what's more, you deserve a glass of wine after your outstanding performance on the platform, not to mention laying on all this,' he told her. 'So drink up, and eat up, and leave handling this mob to me. You've done quite enough for one day, and when all the partying is over, you've still got your young sister to cope with, though I see Toby seems to be dealing with her most adequately at present.'

So he had noticed. And how skilfully he had dealt with Toby's attempted one-upmanship, too. She smiled inwardly—though it would have been nice if he'd actually been cherishing her for her own sake, she thought with mild regret. Even so, she was warmed right through to her bones at his thoughtfulness and caring, and for some reason it was sheer heaven to be sitting here beside him, gulping red wine and scoffing pizza.

What she never guessed was that Grant was in heaven too. He'd dumped Fran's cases in the bedroom, and the truth had dawned blazingly. It was going to be Fran who was sleeping in the second divan, in Kirsty's spare bed. This cottage, the Old Stables, was unmistakably her own home, and not one she shared with Toby. Whatever relationship she and Toby had, it didn't include living together.

Kirsty Holt, here I come.

CHAPTER FOUR

THE next morning—Saturday—when her alarm bleeped its imperious summons, Kirsty would have given anything to be free to switch it off, turn over and go back to sleep.

No way. She had to get cracking. She pushed back her duvet and swung out of bed in one fluid movement, reaching for her towelling robe almost before her eyes had opened. Normally her next action would have been to pull her pink-striped curtains and look across to the cliffs and the frothing sea below, but today there was Fran sleeping at the other end of the room. Kirsty left the curtains drawn. She'd have her own shower, do some preliminary clearing downstairs, and only then think about breakfast. No reason why Fran shouldn't have a lie-in—she'd been travelling most of yesterday.

On her way to the shower, she saw with no surprise that the bedroom remained the muddle it had been the night before, with Fran's gaping cases spilling their contents, and her discarded clothes and shoes scattered around. Fran herself was hidden under her duvet, a hump and a glimpse of gold curls all that was visible.

As she passed, Kirsty placed a gentle hand on the hump, light enough not to rouse her sister. Darling Fran, so seldom with her, but what a delight actually to have her under the same roof. All right, so this was hardly the ideal time to have to try and cope with her and all her drama and excitements, but having her around, however hectic it turned out to be, was never less than fun.

Kirsty had loved Fran from the day she was born, a tiny scrap she could hold in her arms, a successor to the sister she had lost. Julie had gone, with Mum, from the Harley Street house in order to make room for Annabel, though why there wasn't space enough for all of them she hadn't then been able to understand. The Harley Street house was huge, after all, with a basement and five floors above it; there were masses of rooms, even if one floor was entirely given over to consulting-suites, and the basement flat occupied by the receptionist. She had known better, though, than to keep pointing this out—she'd done so once, and seen immediately that it was a disastrous suggestion. Some kind of dreadful *faux pas*. There had been a sudden silence that had vibrated with tension, and eyes had shifted and stared into space. The atmosphere had been unbearable, and Kirsty, at just under eight years old, had taken care never, ever, to repeat her question to anyone at all. But without Mum and Julie she'd felt bereft and alone, and although Dad and Annabel were kind and conscientious, pretending always that they liked having her there with them, she could tell they didn't, not really, and that as far as they were concerned she was a nuisance.

She had retreated from them more and more, going either to the fastness of her own room—previously shared with Julie, so it now seemed painfully empty, even if it was quite nice, as Annabel had kept reiterating, for her to be able to spread her belongings around and do just as she liked—or downstairs to the kitchen, where the housekeeper had allowed her to help with the cooking.

The new baby had been a lifeline. Someone to love and care for, and Kirsty had poured out on to this tiny creature all the love that had been dammed up since Mum and Julie had gone. Looking after Fran, cuddling the warm little bundle, giving her her bottle, helping to bath or change her—all this had brought back warmth and affection into the lonely days. As Kirsty had grown older, and the baby had become a toddler and then a demanding little girl, it had been Kirsty who washed her hands and face before and after meals, changed her, put her to bed, got her up, collected the small garments for the washing machine, and eventually sat with her in the evenings, when Dad and Annabel had been out. She would do her homework in her own room with the door open, and listen out for Fran—the housekeeper would come up and check on them both in mid-evening, and bring Kirsty's supper on a tray, but otherwise they were on their own. Kirsty had revelled in being in charge, and responsible. At last she had her own place, been needed in this house where, until there was Fran to look after, she'd been merely an unwanted third. Now she was useful. Even essential.

Fran had grown up, hardly surprisingly, amazingly like Annabel—unpredictable, easily bored, dashing from one new craze to the next. Like Annabel, too, she needed to be the centre of attention, and if she wasn't, there was trouble.

Trouble, in fact, had blown up as soon as Julie had arrived in Harley Street. Tom Holt had insisted on having her to stay regularly during the school holidays, but there had always been hell to pay with Fran, who had felt displaced, and tried every trick she knew to remedy this. Julie, to be fair to her, hadn't at first resented Fran in the least, but she had soon begun to fight back, and the two of them had soon specialised in telling spiteful stories about one another. Kirsty, though, had loved it when they were both there with her in the house, and ignored the tale-bearing. To this day, she tended to discount whatever Julie told her about Fran, and paid little attention to her repeated injunctions not to stand for Fran's behaviour.

Under the shower this morning, she found that in spite of all the clearing up awaiting her downstairs, she was looking forward joyfully to the day ahead. And what was a bit of tidying, anyway? Nothing. Not when you were fresh after a good night's sleep, exactly as Fran had forecast.

Downstairs shook her resolution. The place, she saw, was a pit.

After everyone had departed the night before, Fran had begged her to come straight to bed. 'Leave all this until the morning—when we're both fresh it won't seem anything. And except for a bit of unpacking, I'll have nothing else to do. Between us, we'll be able to make a clearance in no time.'

Kirsty had demurred. 'I need to move the tables and chairs back into the coach-house early on. They may be wanted over the weekend—they usually are.'

'You can't move them anywhere until we've cleared them, can you? And, anyway, I do absolutely draw the line at traipsing around in the dark heaving them out into the drive and along to the coach-house.'

She had a point there, Kirsty had recognised, and had begun to weaken.

'Anyway,' Fran had continued, 'I'm practically out for the count, and you must be too, though you don't show it, I must say. You look your usual immaculate self, not a hair out of place. How you do it I never have known.'

For some reason, this genuine compliment hadn't pleased Kirsty in the least. Instead it had made her feel unattractive, starchy and, worst of all, thoroughly prissy. And her own hair-style, however controlled, compared with Fran's exuberant golden mop, suddenly seemed only frumpish. Demoralised, she had given in.

'OK, you win. Though I know I'll be sorry tomorrow. I do really loathe coming down to dirty dishes and chaos.'

'Oh, sweetie, do try not to be such a perfectionist. You can stand a bit of mess and muddle for once, can't you? It is the weekend, after all. Don't be like Dad and allow work and the wretched hospital to rule you for ever. Relax. Let go. It'll do you good, you'll see. Anyway, we won't have to manage by ourselves in the morning, Toby promised he'd come round first thing and help us, he swore he would.'

'Oh, did he?' Kirsty had been surprised. Doubtful, too. He hadn't mentioned it to her—but, on the other hand, she'd hardly spoken to him all evening—and in any case, he was a great one for having a long lie-in at weekends if he had the chance.

'He promised faithfully,' Fran had assured her. 'He's fun, isn't he? I could quite go for him, you know. In a big way. And what about the other one, the giant who brought my cases in? He's pretty terrific, too. You never mentioned you had all this talent at St Mark's. I'd have been down like a flash if you'd only said.'

'Never mind, you're here now.' Kirsty had given her a hug. 'And I'm so pleased. But you're right, we're both whacked, so let's go straight to bed this second.'

But now tomorrow was here. She looked around at the shambles, and took a deep breath. The sooner she made a start, the sooner it would be done. She'd make a mug of coffee to wake herself up properly, and then begin.

After a mouthful or two of coffee she felt noticeably stronger, grabbed a bin-bag from her cupboard and started to sweep most of the debris straight into it. Within a quarter of an hour she'd cleared the tables, so she could set about folding the striped tablecloths—which were in fact her sheets from upstairs—ready for the washing machine.

As she drank the last of her coffee, she heard a car crunching across the gravel outside.

Toby? She glanced at her watch. At eight o'clock on a Saturday morning? Miracles did still happen.

She opened the front door, and was confonted by Grant, wearing jeans and a fetching pale blue pullover—he looked terrific. But then, he'd looked terrific in yesterday's formal pin-stripe. Her jaw dropped.

'I wasn't expecting you,' she said abruptly, and at once wished the words unsaid. And it wasn't only her words she would have liked to alter—why hadn't she thought of putting on a bit of make-up after her shower, or done something more interesting with her boring hair than simply yank it back into a pony-tail to keep it out of her way? Pushing these unrewarding emotions hurriedly aside, she pulled the door wide and at last smiled at him and said, 'Do come in, won't you?'

He thought she looked enchanting, and all of fourteen years old. In need of care and protection. Very different from the invulnerable, highly lacquered and poised senior nursing officer he had previously encountered.

'I know it's disgustingly early,' he told her. 'But I was fairly sure, from what you said last night, that you'd be up and about already, organising a grand clear-up. I'm here to help you with that, and then to take you out to breakfast, if you'll come, and I hope you will?'

He was giving her a slanting smile, his dark brows raised interrogatively, his eyes alive with humour and—and something else that she couldn't quite diagnose. Sort of. . .affectionate concern, that was what it was. Just as she'd been astonished to feel before, she found she was just as sure now that she'd be looked after. Nothing could go wrong. Not while he was around.

She gestured at the room. 'I've made a beginning, you see, but it seems a bit awful to expect you to shift this lot for me.'

'It's what I've come for. And you can't do it by yourself, anyway. Where's that sister of yours? Not down?'

'It seemed a shame to wake her—she was out for the count last night—so I thought I'd get started, and—and. . .' He'd offered, hadn't he? So why dither about? Accept with a good grace, and let him get on with it. He needn't have turned up at all, and if he had, it was presumably because he meant what he said, however staggering it might seem to her. 'I've just reached the stage where I certainly need another pair of hands,' she told him honestly. 'And as a matter of fact I am quite keen to get all these tables and chairs back into the coach-house, as they may be needed again. So, if you truly don't mind?'

'Only too glad to help. We had a great evening last night, you know. And what's more, it gave me my first opportunity to talk to the staff off-duty. So I owe you for that, as well as for the splendid meal. It all amounts to a good deal more than I can work off by shifting a few tables and chairs, I assure you.'

'All of us had a good evening, and it was hardly down to me, simply Pizza Express.'

'A good deal more than that, and you know it. So, let's get stuck in.'

With his help, returning the tables and chairs took no more than a quarter of an hour, and she could relock the coach-house and give her mind entirely to restoring her own quarters.

'I'm going to wash up,' Grant informed her, rolling up his sleeves.

'You don't have to,' Kirsty said, with a happy smile. 'This place may be tiny, but it's fantastically well fitted out. We only have to fill the dishwasher.'

'Super. You stack it, then, and I'll bring the stuff through.'

Less than an hour later, Kirsty found herself sitting opposite Grant in the restaurant at Long

Barn—of all fabulous places—while he urged her to order a massive breakfast.

'Bacon, say, and egg of some sort?' he suggested. 'They do very good omelettes, or you could have scrambled egg with smoked salmon.'

Kirsty opened her great grey eyes to their widest extent—which was saying something—and smiled brilliantly at him. He was mesmerised. Clearly, he'd been one hundred per cent right to steal a march on that toad Gresham—though he'd half expected him to be at the Old Stables before him, which he certainly should have been—and insist on dragging Kirsty out for this meal. Not that it hadn't been a struggle to get her here. She'd protested all the way. First of all she'd said no, please, she must give him breakfast, she'd make it at once.

'I had supper here last night, remember?' he'd retorted. 'Now it's my turn to take you for a meal, and it's going to be breakfast—which in fact I've already ordered at Long Barn for nine-thirty. So come along and eat it.'

'But what about poor Fran upstairs?' she'd wailed.

'Poor Fran my foot. She's perfectly comfortable upstairs, and my guess is that all she wants is to sleep the morning away.'

He had been right there, and Kirsty had known it. 'But it seems awful just to go off and leave her. I was going to take her up her breakfast, too.'

'Take her up a cup of tea, then,' he'd said reluctantly. 'You can tell her you're going out at the same time, and say she can go back to sleep until you return. Bet you she'll be delighted, and do just that.'

She'd compromised, made tea and toast, taken both upstairs to the drowsy, somnolent Fran, and delivered her message, while Grant had roamed about downstairs looking at her books.

Fran had half opened one eye, said, 'Tea? Angel. I could sleep for ever. See you later.'

Kirsty had gone downstairs again, and commented, 'You were right—she obviously wants to stay where she is and go back to sleep.'

'My insight is phenomenal,' he had assured her gravely, his eyes glinting. 'Always has been. You wait and see.'

Kirsty had laughed. 'Sounds faintly alarming.'

'Just useful, that's all. Come on, let's go find this breakfast.'

Now they'd found it, and Kirsty was happily drinking freshly squeezed orange juice and eating her way through a plateful of crisp bacon rashers, grilled tomato, sizzling sausage, oozing black field mushrooms and a perfectly fried egg, accompanied by gallons of strong, fragrant coffee. She forgot about being tired. Outside the windows, the sun shone and tiny cotton-wool clouds scurried across a pale blue sky.

'Just the day for a walk along the cliffs,' she commented.

'Why not?' Grant rejoined immediately. 'I'm on, if you are—do us good to walk this meal off.'

She was taken aback. 'Oh, it would be great, wouldn't it?' she agreed. 'But I don't see how I can possibly—I've got to go back and give Fran this breakfast I promised her, for one thing. I can't leave her there to look after herself on her very first morning. And then I simply must go to the shops and get some food in.' She smiled. 'Fran may look ethereal, but she has the appetite of a horse.'

'You seem highly protective,' he told her, his eyes probing. 'Much younger than you, is she?'

'Oh, a lot. I was nearly nine when she was born.'

'Many others in between?'

'Only Julie.'

'So you're the eldest of three—and do you feel you have to look after both your younger sisters?'

'I suppose I do. Always have. But Fran especially. As I said, I was nearly nine when she was born. I did feel fearfully grown up, and she was so tiny. And then, I was always being put in charge of her. I suppose, as I wasn't actually all that old, whatever I may have thought then, I felt awfully important and responsible—in fact, I took I took the job of caring for Fran enormously seriously.'

'And still do,' he informed her. His dark eyes met hers with friendly concern.

She had to smile. 'You're probably right,' she agreed. 'I was conditioned young, after all, and responsibility is part of my make-up now. Both my father and Annabel, my stepmother, were always telling me how much they relied on me, and knew they could depend on me, that kind of thing, so I suppose I accepted the idea that that was how I was meant to be. So it's not surprising I'm still at it.' She gave him a humorous sideways glance, expecting him to smile easily back, but instead, she was startled by the darkness of his expression.

He gave her a look to match it. 'Did no one take any responsibility for you?' he demanded. 'Your stepmother, for instance?'

She chuckled. 'Hardly. Annabel has never been any good at looking after herself, let alone anyone else. Even Dad recognised that. It was why he was everlastingly telling me that if he wasn't there I had to be the one to see to things, stop either Annabel or Fran doing anything really mad.'

'Your father's Tom Holt, people tell me.'

'That's right.' Everyone knew her father by reputation, so it wasn't surprising Grant should be among them. Even so, it made a new bond between them, and somehow it became even easier to share her innermost secrets with him.

'I imagine he must have been away from home a great deal,' Grant was saying.

'I'll say—and of course, often unexpectedly, too. Annabel used to be furious. Fran as well. It's ridiculous, but in those days I used to feel responsible for that, as well. When he let them down by not being at home to take them somewhere, I used to think I ought to make it up to them somehow or other, find some treat to take them on instead. And then, also, I used to want, terribly, to be able to make them see it wasn't his fault he couldn't get home, that this was what his job meant.'

'Did you ever succeed?'

She shook her head. 'Not likely. I sort of knew all along it would be hopeless, even then. Now, of course, I wouldn't bother to try—but when I was younger I was forever working away at it.'

'As well as not being there a lot of the time, was your father difficult when he was at home?' He had a name, Grant knew, for being temperamental in the operating theatre.

'Difficult?' Kirsty seemed surprised. 'Not in the least. When he was there he was super. We all adored him—still do, I have to say.' Suddenly the great grey eyes were brilliant with unshed tears, and she looked agonised. She blinked momentarily, and then went on determinedly, 'It was just that he hardly ever was there.' She smiled, heart-rendingly, Grant thought. To him she seemed more beautiful than ever, and unutterably precious, so that he longed to be able to enfold her in his own strong arms, and keep her safe.

This was the point, he reminded himself, to stop dreaming. To get right away from Kirsty's personal life, to return to the work they shared. He must start talking about the problems of the Community Care Service, and begin to discuss patients' problems. Instead, he heard himself say, with the utmost gentleness, 'Tell me about your childhood. This is your stepmother you've been mentioning, Annabel, so what happened to your own mother?'

'Oh, she died when I was tiny—before I could talk. I don't think I actually remember her, though of course I've seen plenty of photographs.'

'So it was your stepmother who brought you up?'

'That's right—my first stepmother, not Annabel. Cathy, in fact, though mostly I tend to call her Mum, which is how I still think of her.' To confide in this man was for some reason the most natural thing in the world, and telling him about her family and upbringing was amazingly comforting. From the first moment she'd set eyes on him, of course, although professionally he'd been not merely commanding but oddly alarming, she'd had this absolute certainty that she could trust him for ever.

'So your present stepmother is your father's third wife?' he was enquiring, an odd expression in his eyes. He was thinking that this explained some of the remarks made about Tom Holt.

'That's right. My first stepmother had been his theatre sister, and a great friend of my mother's. He married her very quickly after my mother died, to be a mother to me, and to give me brothers and sisters.'

'And how did—er—Cathy feel about this, do you know?'

'Oh, she was quite open about it from the beginning. She said Dad adored my mother, theirs was a true love-story, and her death more or less destroyed him at the time, and he believed he'd never love anyone again in that way, so he and Cathy married for friendship, and family life. They knew they got on well, and could work together, and she'd been, as I said, a great friend of my mother's, which meant I took her for granted—she'd always been in and out of the house.'

This was the type of companionable marriage Julie, Cathy's daughter, had made, and which she was always urging on Kirsty. It was why she wanted Kirsty to stop dithering about and marry Toby. But Kirsty had never stopped believing that there must be more to marriage than merely an easy companionship and the successful upbringing of children. 'Personally,' she heard herself say, much to her surprise, 'I think Cathy loved Dad to distraction, and always has, though she's never admitted it. She was the perfect partner for him, anyway, I still think, but of course, quite the opposite of what he'd expected, he had to go and fall in love again.' And that, she'd always realised, was what could easily happen, if you decided to make a so-called sensible marriage for companionship. What if you fell for someone else? 'Annabel simply bowled Dad over, she came storming into his life, and that was the end of his marriage to Cathy. From then on everything changed, he and Mum split up, she and Julie left, and Dad married Annabel and had Fran.'

'That seems very hard on everyone except Annabel and your father,' was all Grant allowed himself to say, though inwardly he was furiously angry with Tom Holt, ruining the lives of three people for what needed to be no more than a momentary affair with a feather-headed blonde—here, of course, he was seeing Fran on the previous evening, he realised, but he was ready to hazard a guess that mother and daughter were alike as two peas.

'It was awful,' Kirsty agreed. 'Mum and Julie just went, left the house in Harley Street and moved with all their belongings to the weekend cottage, while I had to stay on in the house with Annabel, who scared me out of my mind. Mum was small, dark and cuddly. Not exactly glamorous, I can see now, looking back, but always there for us, while Annabel—well, she was blonde and fashionable, like a being from another planet, as far as I was concerned. I was terrified of her—probably she was scared stiff of me. After all, there I was, stuck with her in the house which had always been my home, resenting her and the break-up of the marriage, not understanding it and longing for Mum and Julie to come home, for everything to be as it had been before. I can't have been the easiest stepdaughter, and she can't actually have been much older than Fran is now. But naturally, none of that crossed my mind at the time.' She shook her head, her huge eyes filled with sadness for all of them.

Grant could have drowned in them. At the same time he wanted to hold her tightly, assure her she was all right now and he was going to take care of her for the rest of her days, nothing awful would happen to her again.

She was shaking her head. 'Broken families are hell all round, aren't they?' she asked.

'You can say that again,' he agreed heavily. He made an effort at this stage, for safety's sake, to divert the conversation away from the two of them and into a discussion about the broken homes of too many of their small patients, and the problems they had ahead of them as a result. But the effort failed, and instead, to his astonishment, he blurted out, 'I'm as guilty as anyone, you know. My own marriage came to a sticky end inside five years.' There, he'd made his confession, got it off his chest. He scowled at the tablecloth, not wanting, any longer, to meet her eyes.

All at once he looked years older, and dreadfully tired, Kirsty saw with anguish. He was plainly so unhappy that she longed to be able to comfort him, if only she could. But it wasn't her love and support he needed, it was someone else's, that of the unknown wife he'd lost. He must have been so deeply hurt, and she ached for him. All she said was, 'What went wrong?'

He shrugged. 'It just disintegrated. Fell apart. We'd honestly started out with high hopes, both of us—or that's what I imagined at the time, anyway—but it somehow went bad on us, and we couldn't speak without hurting each other. Deliberately, too, not by any kind of accident. We became totally destructive. I'm not proud of myself.'

'What actually happened?' Kirsty asked softly.

He laughed shortly. 'I suppose you might say ambition happened. Both of us—we'd married as students, you see—had to chase jobs up and down the country, and the result was we were lucky if we spent one weekend together in three months. I did try to do something about it. I took a registrar's post that wasn't the one I really coveted or needed, simply so that we could work in the same hospital and share a flat again. I thought Natalie'd be grateful, and pleased, too. Instead, she seemed mainly surprised, and a bit put out. And gradually I took in what was going on. She was heavily into an affair with her own consultant.'

Kirsty was stunned. 'Oh, how could she?' she exclaimed. 'How perfectly awful for you.'

'She took the line that I was making a fuss about nothing. I hadn't been there, and the affair had been fun, as well as useful. It would end automatically when her job ended, I didn't own her body, there was such a thing as open marriage, and the demands of our careers had to come first with both of us. Then she had a chance of a good post at the other end of the country, she just took off, and that was that. There I was, stuck with this job I hadn't wanted in the first place, feeling every sort of fool, and with this malevolent consultant of Natalie's feeling bad too, and taking it out on me whenever he got the chance. So we divorced, and that was that. I don't know why I'm dripping on about it this morning—it's all in the past, and I've put it behind me. But I can't say I'm proud of it.' He met her eyes at last, and gave her the sideways, slanting smile she was coming to love. 'Could have done better,' he added lightly.

'She could have done better,' Kirsty said hotly. 'This Natalie person. If you ask me.' Natalie was a horrid name, Kirsty decided unreasonably.

'More coffee?' This time Grant succeeded in changing the subject. What could she be thinking of him, moaning away at breakfast, of all meals, the start of the day, about his failed marriage? But he didn't want to let her go. Not yet. Not ever, if he was honest.

'Coffee? Er—no, thank you. I've had masses—frightfully good coffee, isn't it?' He was changing the subject. He was wishing he hadn't told her anything about his private life and his marriage—perhaps he thought she'd rush round the hospital telling everyone. As if she would. She'd die rather than breathe a word. Struggling to regain her scattered wits, to make sense, she went on about the breakfast. 'It's been an absolutely super meal altogether,' she enthused. 'Thank you so much—I'm really set up for the day. It's been truly great. And now I really should get back home, and see to Fran and the weekend shopping.'

'Sure you won't come for that walk on the cliffs first?' he asked. He couldn't bear to lose her yet. He wanted to talk to her all day.

But she refused, as he'd known she would.

'At least let me drive you to the supermarket,' he urged. 'And anywhere else you need for your shopping. Then I'll take you home, and you can see to that sister of yours.' He gave her the slanting smile again. 'Though I'm bound to point out that, if she's reached her twentieth year, you, as a good elder sister, should be training her to stand on her own two feet, not ministering to her and pandering to her every whim.'

'You sound just like my sister Julie,' she told him joyously. Having Grant take a hand in her family life was great. 'And I'm sure you're both right. I'll have to try it out one day.'

'One day soon,' he advised, his dark eyes glinting. 'Like tomorrow.'

'Tomorrow absolutely anything might happen,' she said radiantly.

CHAPTER FIVE

WHEN Grant drove Kirsty back to Highcliffe after her shopping, they found the drive outside the coach-house bustling with activity, cars and vans coming and going, decanting their contents into eager hands. The big doors of the coach-house were fastened back, and inside, the trestle-tables had been set up in an open rectangle, and groups of helpers were vociferously engaged in setting out assorted objects—china, glass, pots and pans, electrical goods, materials, linen, clothing of every kind from overcoats to nightdresses.

'Another jumble sale,' Kirsty commented. 'Thank the lord we got everything back in time.' She checked. 'No, it's not any deity I should be thanking. It's you. Without your arrival, I doubt if I'd have managed it. And thank you again for that great breakfast, and the lift, and your help with the shopping.' She smiled brilliantly into his dark eyes—by now she felt as if they had known one another for ever.

'My pleasure,' he told her, mesmerised by the smile, and searching wildly and in vain for a reason to stay on until darkness fell. Instead, he carried her shopping to the door of the Old Stables, turned on his heel, got into his Volvo and drove off with a casual wave.

Kirsty let herself in, suddenly deflated. The house was empty, silent. Deserted. No sign of Fran upstairs, either, though the bedroom looked as if a hurricane had struck. Familiar with the effect, Kirsty deduced that Fran had dressed in a rush to go out somewhere. So she needn't have bothered to buy the turkey and ham pie with cranberries, that Fran adored, for lunch. No matter, it would keep. She'd stash the food away and then have yoghurt and an apple herself, all she needed after her huge breakfast.

On the kitchen counter she found a note from Toby. He'd called, it said, intending to take her and Fran out to lunch. 'But Fran tells me you've been gone since dawn, with Grant, of all people, so rather than leave your sister all on her own I'm taking her to lunch. See you later.'

Annoyance blazed out at her from the scrawl. Toby was offended, and making it clear, as usual. But it had not been Toby, but Grant, who had turned up at eight in the morning to help with the clearing up, Grant who had dealt with the tables and chairs, moved them across to the coach-house and stacked them there. Toby, however, plainly felt that not only had he every right to be disgruntled because she hadn't waited in, but apparently considered she was neglecting Fran.

Toby was jealous of Grant, of course, that was all it was, and he was taking it out on her. But he'd gone too far. She'd had enough. Maybe this was only a straw in the wind, but it happened to be the last straw.

Finish. This was the end.

Not, of course, the end of their long friendship, far too well established to disintegrate over any minor tiff. But the end of any shared future.

She was irritated with him because of his silly note, naturally, but underlying that was another feeling, much deeper and more meaningful. What was it?

Relief. She had to recognise it. A niggling rejection of any future with Toby had been eating away at her for months, but at last it was settled. She had made up her mind. Friendship for as long as he wanted it, but not marriage. Not ever, no matter how many consultant posts and houses swam into view. She could relax, ignore what friends and relations told her. Marriage was not on. There would be no wedding-bells pealing for her and Toby.

Briskly, she began putting her purchases away into the fridge and freezer and the vegetable racks, and thought about the evening meal. Presumably Toby would be returning for it—that would be what he meant by seeing her later, and he'd hardly propose taking them both out, if he'd already given Fran lunch.

She'd do a casserole in the slow cooker, so that it would be ready at whatever time the two of them came in. She'd felt extravagant and bought venison, to celebrate Fran's arrival. She'd do it with red wine, as there were several part-bottles left from yesterday's party. Mushrooms, too, and lentils. They could have it with baked potatoes.

Soon there was an enticing aroma of wine, onions, mushrooms and braising venison, and Kirsty put the lid on the slow cooker and went upstairs to change.

The bedroom, of course, remained shambolic. She did a fast job of hurling Fran's discarded clothes and cases into her capacious cupboards, hanging amazingly filmy sheer garments alongside her own more sturdy—and far less alluring—tweeds, sweaters and jeans.

Another shower, and then she pulled on her favourite evening wear, a velour tracksuit, once a striking cherry, now, much-washed, a soft rose-pink. She tied a silk scarf in an Indian print of the same shades round her neck, and made up her face with a good deal of care. After having to display this morning's scrubbed-clean look to Grant when she would so much have appreciated feeling her best, she wasn't going to greet Fran's critical eyes with a shiny nose and pale lips. She wasn't planning to go out, so she left her hair loose, and it hung pale and gleaming below her shoulders. It would get in the way, but after all, she'd done most of the cooking.

Perhaps she should have it cut? She turned her head, dissatisfied, glancing at herself from different angles. It might be quite an idea to have it cut fashionably short. Easy to manage, and she could afford, with her new salary, to have it done regularly.

Suddenly she tired of all this self-examination. She knew what had provoked it. Fran. She was always critical of what she was apt to call Kirsty's dowdy looks, and whenever they were together would run a campaign to bring her up to date fashionwise. But there was no need whatever to anticipate like this, and after all, Kirsty reminded herself fairly, Fran was terrific on clothes, make-up and hair-style. Her advice was worth having, she could be inspired—even if what she advocated might often be impractical for a hard-working nurse spending long hours in children's wards. She must ask Fran, though, what she thought about her hair, about cutting it short.

She hadn't seen Mrs Anstruther today. There would be just time to pop in and have a quick word with her before she needed to expect Fran and Toby back. She jumped up and shot downstairs.

Mrs Anstruther was Kirsty's landlady, and the sole remaining member of the family to live in the great Victorian pile. Now in her late eighties, she had been widowed twenty years earlier, her daughter had told Kirsty, and they wanted her to sell the great unmanageable house and live with them in Nottingham. 'But her whole life is in Halchester, and we had to accept that moving her wouldn't really be kind, simply a move for the sake of our own peace of mind, so she stays on here alone, and we try to come as often as we can. But we don't see nearly enough of her, I'm afraid.' She'd gone on to ask if Kirsty could make a point of dropping in on her fairly often, just to make sure she was all right.

'No problem,' Kirsty had said at once. Nor was it. She liked Mrs Anstruther, a lively old soul with a humorous eye and a fund of tales of earlier days in Halchester.

'I can easily look in most days, if it would relieve your mind.'

'Oh, if you could, it would be such a relief. You wouldn't need to do anything for her, she's perfectly capable. It's just that if I knew you were keeping an eye out it would make all the difference. Look, I'll give you our telephone number—don't hesitate to ring if you have the faintest doubt. That's absolutely all I'm asking, so don't feel you're in the least responsible for actually doing anything. It would be such a comfort to know you're here on the spot and you'll keep in touch.'

Kirsty had thought little more about it. Her daily round was filled with people—children, parents, staff—and to add one elderly lady on the other side of the drive was no sort of burden. She looked in on her way to or from the hospital, occasionally—not often—did some shopping for her, or climbed up on a stepladder to replace a light bulb. However, in due course a letter had arrived from Mrs Anstruther's daughter and her husband, formally thanking her for her kindness, and telling her that they were reducing the rent by half. 'We both feel this is the least we can do, and we have instructed the agent accordingly, as from the first of this month.'

Kirsty had been shaken, and had first wanted to refuse their offer, but Toby had told her to grab the money and be thankful. 'If you ask me, you're entitled to it—you do enough for the old girl.'

'Hardly a thing,' Kirsty had protested. But Emma had agreed with Toby, and even Fieldy, when approached, had thought she should accept the rent reduction.

'You're doing them a valuable service, after all. A trained eye as well as a helping hand, and on the spot. They'd probably be embarrassed and in a quandary if you turn them down.'

So Kirsty had written to thank them, and gone straight out to buy the limed pine dining-table she'd been yearning for.

Recently she had managed to persuade Mrs Anstruther, who was more frail than she cared to admit, to accept some help with the housework, and had found a placement with her for one of the former Northcliffe cleaners.

This evening she let herself in through the kitchen

door as usual, and found the old lady drinking sherry in her conservatory.

She was offered a glass as soon as she appeared, and took it, knowing how much Mrs Anstruther enjoyed sharing her evening ritual.

'I hope the noise and the comings and goings last night didn't disturb you too much,' Kirsty said.

'My dear, you know I like activity around here—I can deceive myself into imagining this place is the hub of the universe. In any case, it's the Save the Children bazaar and jumble sale in the coach-house all day tomorrow, so I'm afraid you'll have to put up with all that on your day off.'

'It won't worry me—I'm like you, plenty going on is how I like it. And I wanted to tell you, I've my sister Fran staying, so if you see someone around when I'm on duty, that's who it'll be. I hope she won't be a nuisance—she's not exactly a quiet little mouse.'

'You must bring her in when you have a minute. I'd love to meet her.'

Kirsty promised she'd do this, and they both sat drinking sherry and admiring the sunset over the water, until Kirsty said goodbye and went back to check on her casserole.

While she was doing this, the telephone rang. Dinah Hayward, her junior sister in charge of the new service for the weekend.

'I'm sorry to bother you at home, but I really do need to have a word with you, if you aren't in the middle of anything wildly important.'

'No, it's quite OK. Go ahead.'

'We seem to have problems with the Weybourne family.'

'Oh, *no*. I was really thinking that was one family where everything was going swimmingly.'

'We have a problem, but quite likely it's merely temporary. I've just got back from seeing them—I'm in the office—and I thought, if you could bear it, it would clear my mind. The problem is actually mainly psychological, if you ask me. However, the ostensible reason for sending for me was that they've all—except Linda and Kevin, so far—got terrible fluey colds, with high temperatures and loads of coughing and spluttering non-stop. They're trying to keep their germs away from Linda, but Jill Weybourne is sneezing and dripping herself, and should obviously be tucked up in bed, not dashing round the house looking after everyone. They've all kept well away from Linda, I'm told, and so they should, though this does mean, of course, that she's confined to her own room. Kevin Weybourne is able to look after her, with the volunteers, over the weekend while he's not at work, and so far he hasn't developed any symptoms, though I'd guess it's only a matter of hours before he goes down too. Linda's perfectly all right so far, but the trouble is, she's panicking. She seems absolutely terrified that she'll pick up this respiratory infection, and she wants back inside St Mark's fastest.'

'I don't blame her one bit. She's so vulnerable to infections, and a lung infection is the last thing she should risk. But what's the difficulty? Why not take her in? It's easy enough to arrange, even if it needs a bit of organising at either end—but I assume if it was that simple you wouldn't be ringing me.'

'That's right. That would be straightforward, merely time-consuming, what with a bed, and apparatus, an ambulance to bring her in, and all her volunteers and helpers to be notified. Nothing in it, though. The trouble is, Jill Weybourne doesn't agree to re-admission. She says Linda can perfectly well go on being looked after at home, safe in her own room and bathroom, away from infection, especially as Kevin can see to her over the weekend. She says Linda's hyping it up for her own ends, she's not really scared, she just wants attention. She's never before, Jill maintains, been just an ordinary member of the family and, at the moment, the least in need. She's been the only one with a medical problem, the centrepiece, and now she won't wear the others being the ones in need of tender loving care, so she wants out, back to where she'll have a team seeing to her needs. It's a try-on, Jill says, and to give in to her would be fatal. Linda's been having a good deal of difficulty in adapting to being an ordinary member of the family, instead of the one suffering alone in hospital, and this is her chance to get back.'

'That may well be true, of course. It's only a stage we all foresaw. An inevitable stage, once all the excitement of being welcomed home and having her new bedroom and bathroom wore off, we knew she was bound to discover the disadvantages of being one of three daughters at home, instead of the only one in hospital, being visited by her devoted family. All natural enough.'

'Absolutely. It was going to happen at some point, but Jill is adamant that if we give in to her now, it'll be a real set-back. She'll have got her own way, and she'll do it again.'

'Perhaps. And perhaps not. But it seems to me she has every justification for being scared about infection getting to her lungs—she can't count on being able to breathe unaided at the best of times. It's a learned skill, no longer automatic—why is there a respirator ready at her bedside, after all? That's not psychological, that's a very real physical danger, and she knows it. She's experienced it. I'm not the least surprised she's dead scared. All the same, you're right, it is dicey. I'm glad you rang me. We're in one of those no-win situations, aren't we? What do we do when the patient wants admission, but the mother doing the caring wants to go on doing it? And Linda is still only thirteen.'

'But it's Linda who's the patient, isn't it?'

'And the patient has to come first, when in doubt? You've a point—on the other hand, the caring mum is at the centre of the new service, and Linda's mum Jill is one of the best. Policy-wise, I'm behind Jill, every step. Nursing-wise, I'm behind Linda. When in doubt, do whatever's best for the patient.'

'Rule of thumb we've all been trained to rely on. I know what I haven't mentioned so far—it wasn't Jill who rang in, it was Kevin. On Jill's behalf, because he thinks she should be in bed herself, not running round the house like a fiend out of hell trying to cook, feed and nurse the lot of them.'

'So Kevin wants Linda admitted for the sake of the family, Linda herself wants admission because she's afraid of what will happen if she stays at home, whereas Jill wants her to remain at home for the sake—as she sees it—of her psychological health. If we forget about all the emotions for a moment, numerically it's two to one.'

'Come again? You've lost me.'

'Linda wants admission, Kevin wants admission.

It's only Jill who's standing out against it, and she's in the throes of this cold.'

'So you think we should go ahead and bring her in?'

'It's to play safe. Tell you what, how about if I meet you there, and we decide on the spot, with the family?'

'That would be the greatest—but I'm truly sorry to break up your Saturday night like this.'

'What I'm here for. I'll meet you there in about twenty minutes or half an hour, OK?' Dinah thanked her, Kirsty put the telephone down, replaced the lid on the slow cooker, turned it to low, and scribbled a note for Fran.

When she reached the council estate on the other side of Halchester where the Weybournes lived, Dinah's car was already parked outside the house, and Kirsty went in to join her. In the hall she found, for the first time in her dealings with this family, the two parents locked in confrontation.

'Never mind Linda, she's not the point today, the point is Jill simply can't carry on. And shouldn't.' Kevin was forcefully addressing Dinah, herself barely over the front step.

'I can still speak for myself, thank you very much,' his wife asserted, though hoarsely. 'When I can't carry on, I'll say so. And I know what's best for my own daughter.'

'You have two other daughters, don't forget. And yourself. And you're not fit to carry on like this.'

'You don't look at all well, Jill,' Kirsty put in. She wasn't sure the two Weybournes had even noticed her arrival in the narrow hall.

This was borne out by the look of utter surprise

Jill Weybourne gave her. The surprise was quickly followed by reproach, and then accusation, as she exclaimed, 'Surely *you* can't suppose I'm not capable of caring for Linda?'

'Of course you're capable,' Kirsty assured her. 'But you're running a temperature yourself, I can see that from here, and you ought to be in bed. If you allow yourself to get really ill, you certainly won't be helping Linda, or your family.' Jill's high colour and brilliant eyes, she was assuming, were not the result of temper alone.

'Isn't that what I've been telling her all day?' Kevin exploded. 'Much good it will do Linda or any of us if she goes down with pneumonia.'

'It would be very bad for Linda if we give in to her now.' Jill moved back to what for her was the main point.

'And it will be bad for you and the rest of the family if we keep her here when you're not fit. You should be in bed, and I can't manage Linda as well as the rest of you,' Kevin told her. He turned to Kirsty. 'When we agreed to have her at home, it was on the understanding that you'd take her in at once if we needed it—not just if she was worse herself, but if for any reason we felt we couldn't manage. That's what you promised us, you and that Dr Field-Dalling. You said so again and again. Well, we can't manage now, I'm telling you so, and asking you to take her back in.'

'And I'm asking you not to.' Jill glared at her husband. 'Kev, I *know* it's wrong for her if we do this. We're playing into her hands, and we'll pay for it later. This is the moment we have to stand firm.'

'This is the moment when we have to think about

the well-being of the whole family, and you in particular, instead of putting Linda first, no matter what. You never think about the rest of us, only about Linda. It's not right, and I'm not putting up with it any longer. I want Linda back in, Miss Holt, and that's a formal request.'

'Which I accept,' Kirsty told him. While the altercation went on, she'd taken her decision. 'We'll take Linda straight in. And you must go to bed, Jill, and think of yourself, for once, as your husband says. You're not fit to be up at all, let alone looking after anyone.'

'You haven't even bloody seen her,' Jill retorted furiously. Her voice was failing her, but her body expressed the anger she felt. 'You're just siding with Kev against me. I'm the one who knows what's best for our Linda—I look after her all the time.'

'Of course you do, and you're worn out just now, and thoroughly unwell yourself. What you need is bed, and being looked after. I'm taking Linda in because of you, not because of her. This time she has to come second, and you must come first. What we said, when we decided about Linda coming home, was that we'd take her back in at any time, if she needed it, or if caring for her at home was too much for you.'

'It's not too much for me, I keep telling you,' Jill persisted, and burst into angry tears, sobs battling with coughing and snorting, culminating in an explosive sneeze.

They'd be lucky, Kirsty thought, if they didn't all go down with the Weybourne cold in the coming weeks. 'I'll see Linda now,' she told both parents, 'and explain what's happening. In the meantime,

Dinah, if you'd go on ahead and get the bed lined up for her and send the ambulance on its way, I'll follow with the patient.'

An hour later she was driving to St Mark's behind the ambulance containing Linda, her wheelchair, and Kevin. At the hospital, Dinah had organised the bed and was there with a student nurse ready to install Linda.

Her father at once said he'd be off. 'If you don't mind, Miss Holt, I won't stick around. Linda's OK here with you, and I'd like to get back to the wife and the other kids. You can be dead sure that obstinate Jill won't have thought of going to bed yet, she'll be starting on the washing-up instead, or making hot drinks all round. So I'll be off, and thank you for taking Linda in. I'm sorry if I was a bit stroppy, like, earlier, but I was that worried.'

'Jill was doing far too much, and you were quite right to ask us to have Linda back here for a while. This is what our new scheme is for, to take the pressure off home if it's necessary, for whatever reason. In any case, it's not just Jill. We can't risk Linda getting a chesty cold, can we?'

'Well, that's what I thought, but Jill——'

'She's got a rotten cold, she feels terrible, and she's lost her sense of proportion. Now, how are you going to get back? I could try and get them to rustle up some transport for you, but it is Saturday night, and you might have a bit of a wait.'

'No, I'll be fine. I can pick up a bus at the corner, and after that it's only a bit of a walk, and I reckon I can do with some time to meself to get calmed down and ready to tackle Jill. Otherwise I'll just walk straight back into a blazing row, which is what

Jill's going to want, and I'm not having, if I can just hang on to me temper, like.'

'Off you go, then, and the best of luck. And you can tell Jill, if it would help, that I said straight to bed and no argument.' She gave him the blinding smile that so transformed her, and in the midst of his anxieties Kevin Weybourne had a strong urge to hug her.

Instead, he returned to his daughter, kissed her, and enquired, 'All right then, pet? I'll come in and see you in the morning.'

Linda looked at him, large-eyed. 'All right, Dad. Don't bother to come in the morning if you're too busy seeing to the others. I shan't mind.' It was plain to everyone that she would mind very much indeed, that she adored her father, and that to earn his approval was what counted most.

'Don't you worry, I'll be here, you can be sure of it, though I may not be able to stay long.'

'No problem.' Linda was airy. 'You put Mum straight to bed when you get home,' she added anxiously.

'I'll do that, pet,' her father said. 'See you tomorrow, then.'

Linda's eyes followed her father across the ward and out through the swing doors, remaining fixed on them after he had disappeared. Kirsty watched her, and a new idea crossed her mind. What if Linda had not been playing up at home to attract attention, as her mother imagined? What if, instead, she had been loyally furthering her father's efforts to get her back into hospital so that her mother could rest?

Exploring this theory, she remarked to Linda, 'I think, with any luck, we'll have brought you back in here before you had a chance to pick up this infection that's going round your family, so that's good, isn't it?'

'I never thought I'd caught it, actually. It was Mum who was bad, not me. And she wore a mask whenever she came into my room, from the very start of the tickle in her throat, just in case, she said. Anyway, from when he came home yesterday, it's been Dad who's been seeing to me—Mum hasn't been into my room since then.'

'That was sensible of them both. And perhaps now he'll get home and persuade your mother to go to bed and have a real rest.'

'So it was a really good idea for me to come in, wasn't it?' Linda demanded, clearly in need of reassurance on this point.

No doubt she'd followed the ins and outs of the shouting match outside her door, Kirsty reflected. 'I'm sure it was absolutely the right thing for your mother. She'll be able to rest and take care of herself, and then when your father goes back to work on Monday, she'll be a bit better and ready to carry on.'

'And anyway, she'll only have the other two to look after, not me as well.'

'It's possible they'll all be better by then. It's a nasty cold they've got, but it may not last long.'

'Dad may have got it, by then,' Linda said gloomily.

'Well, he may, that's true.' Was she worried about this, or was she intimating that her stay in the ward needed to be prolonged? Time would show. 'We'll just have to wait and see, shan't we?' she added, as much to herself as Linda. 'Now, I think you're about ready to be settled for the night, don't you? Would you like a hot drink or anything first?'

'Horlicks? Could I have some Horlicks?'

Linda had always enjoyed a mug of Horlicks, Kirsty remembered. 'Just the job,' she agreed warmly.

At this point Dinah returned from seeing Linda's father off—they'd presumably been chatting about the situation in the Weybourne household, Kirsty realised. She and Dinah must have a chat about that set-up.

It was not to be yet, however. Dinah made this clear with absolute firmness. 'I'll take over now,' she said. 'You get off home, Kirsty, and thanks for all the help.'

'No problem. See you on Monday, then, if not before.' She crossed her fingers, Dinah did likewise, and shook her head, too. 'Bye, Linda, have a good night. Oh, and I just promised her some Horlicks, Dinah.'

'Right, I'll see to it.'

For a moment, Kirsty was ready to tell her not to bother, she'd go into the kitchen herself and make Horlicks for all of them—maybe buttered toast, too. She was ravenous. But she didn't say anything, simply walked away down the ward and out into the passage, along towards the lifts.

Again, she changed her mind. She wasn't going to stand there, pressing buttons and waiting for a recalcitrant lift with a hopelessly erratic memory. She turned aside, and began running downstairs.

She'd gone down two flights when suddenly there was a rush of feet behind her, and a peremptory voice demanding, 'What on earth do you think you're doing here on what's supposed to be your weekend off?'

Startled—she had had no notion Grant was anywhere in the department, let alone behind her on the stairs—she turned to face him, her heart lifting at the mere sight of his large frame towering over her. One side of her longed to say, 'How lovely—you're here,' and then fling her arms round him, tell him all about Linda and the Weybournes, and ask anxiously, 'Do you think we did the right thing? Or not? I've been a bit worried.' But even as she was aching to pour out her gratitude for his arrival on the scene just when she needed him, another side of her was rebelling furiously. How feeble could she be? She spoke sternly to herself. You've admitted Linda, it was the right thing to do and you know it. You do not, repeat, not need Grant Sheringham to approve it and stand by ready to prop up your fragile morale every time you take a difficult decision. Surely you can trust your own judgement? Well, yes, of course she could. But it was lovely to have him here, at the end of this long day. Her eyes melting, she looked up at him and answered his enquiry with apparent serenity.

'I came in to admit Linda Weybourne—if I'd known you were already on the scene, I'd have asked your opinion.' That was as far as she was prepared to go. 'What are you doing here, anyway?'

'I'm on call for Fieldy this weekend, and I got summoned to Casualty for an asthmatic of his. I admitted her, so Quentin and I have been up there with her in the ward for some time.' Quentin, newly qualified and in his first job, rushed, anxious and noticeably timid, though, they'd been assured, quite bright, was the houseman, the most junior doctor on the ward. 'I've left Quentin to see to the patient now, and I was just departing when I spotted you ahead of me, so I came to see what was up.' He knew he was talking for the sake of talking, waffling, not wanting to walk away from her.

She gave him her transforming smile. 'It's been a long day for you, then,' she said sympathetically.

He was transfixed. She was incredible. Sometimes so formal and stand-offish, but then suddenly, like now, all the barriers would go down and she'd be so heart-rendingly tender and concerned that it was a struggle not to take her straight into his arms and claim her for a lifetime. He could hardly do that here, but he could at least postpone his departure—ask her about this patient she'd admitted, for instance.

Two minds with a single thought, and by a split second Kirsty got there first. 'If you've got a moment,' she suggested, 'we could go into the office, have some coffee——' somehow she felt it would be too juvenile to offer him Horlicks '—and I could tell you about Linda—I'd be so glad to hear what you think.' Then, conscience-stricken, she remembered he'd been called out to Casualty, that he'd come up to the ward with the patient, been there for the lord only knew how long admitting her with Quentin, and now here she was, holding him up when all he was longing for was to get away. 'Oh, no,' she added in a panic, 'you're trying to leave. It's perfectly all right. I'm not actually worried about Linda, she'll keep.'

This was his opportunity, and he took it. 'You must want to leave too,' he told her. 'Why don't we do it together, this minute?' He could take her out for a meal. But they'd had breakfast this morning, he reminded himself. She'd hardly want to end a long day—that it had certainly been—exactly as she'd begun it, eating with him. Never mind. He could but try. 'Have you eaten?'

'Eaten?' she repeated, startled. She must sound like a gramophone, she realised. He'd think her a complete fool, standing there repeating what he said.

'Yes.' He was grinning broadly.

He looked like a mischievous boy, and she wanted to kiss him.

'You know,' he went on, making gestures of raising food to his mouth and chewing vigorously.

The kids on the ward would adore him if he went on like this often. The kids on the ward? She adored him. She chuckled happily. 'Yes, I do know what you mean. Dimwitted I may be, but eating I recognise nearly always. No, I haven't eaten—not really since I had that super breakfast with you this morning, I don't think. I was too full after that for lunch, so I had yoghurt mid-afternoon, and that was about it.'

'I had a sandwich around three, but I haven't had anything since, either, so how about coming back with me to Long Barn and having dinner? How does that strike you?' Please God, let her say yes.

'Two meals in one day at Long Barn? That's pushing it a bit,' she told him.

She hadn't actually turned him down. Press on. 'If it wasn't Saturday night, so that everywhere will be packed out, I'd suggest somewhere different,' he explained apologetically.

This wasn't what she'd meant at all, as she began to explain.

He cut through her protestations. 'Point is,' he said, 'I ordered the meal there before I left, and there'll be a table waiting, so it would be simplest to go straight there. Do join me.' He looked hopefully at her, and added for good measure, 'We could talk about Linda, too. You could tell me what's been happening, and why you got called out.'

'Well,' she said dubiously.

Praise be, she was wavering, she wasn't turning him down flat—which, to be honest, was what he'd expected. 'I need to come back here to have another look at this asthmatic, Zoe, last thing, so I could drive you over to Long Barn now, we could have a meal, and then I'd drive you back here and you could pick up your own car and be off.'

Kirsty was thinking about Fran, and Toby, and the casserole. But suddenly she switched off. Fitting everyone in was too complicated. The food was there, Fran and Toby could eat it together and good luck to them. Both of them would enjoy it, Toby because he was clearly smitten by her sister, and Fran because from a small child she'd revelled in showing off to Kirsty's friends. For herself, she was opting out and grabbing a good offer while it was there.

'That would be great,' she announced, with a ravishing smile. 'I'd love it. And I'm famished.'

Grant could hardly believe his luck. 'Let's go,' he said urgently, beginning to hustle her away down the stairs before she had a chance to change her mind.

Unexpectedly, she was aghast. 'I—I can't possibly go looking like this. I'm not dressed for Long Barn.' She pointed feverishly at the faded rose tracksuit, remembering, too, her mussed-up hair and by now non-existent make-up.

'You look terrific,' he assured her. Seldom had he been more certain of anything. 'It doesn't matter what you wear, in any case. I won't say you'll pass unnoticed, because you won't. You look far too good for that.'

Crazily, she believed him. If Grant told her she looked terrific, then terrific was how she looked. No problem. Her spirits rose sky-high, and she gave him the mesmerising smile he treasured. 'Just let me do something about my face,' she said. 'And I'll be with you.'

'Come exactly as you are,' he said firmly, taking her soft rose-clad arm and propelling her down the stairs fast. 'If we stick around here for another second, someone will grab one of us for some emergency—you know it as well as I do. Do your face in the Long Barn cloakroom, if you must. But for now, let's get out of here.'

Twenty minutes later they were seated opposite one another at the same table they'd occupied nearly twelve hours ago, and Grant was once again seeking her approval to order mouth-watering dishes.

It wasn't the food, though, that transported Kirsty into this brilliant enchantment. She was remembering how, on that first occasion she and Grant had met, at the ward round one afternoon in Northcliffe, she'd been seized by the same illogical certainty that comfort and joy were to be found wherever Grant was. Forever. Security and enduring love, too. For sure.

She'd thought this certainty mad then. It was still mad today. Complete lunacy. But it happened to be true. And inescapable. She had fallen in love with Grant.

How right she'd been through all these years to go on insisting, in spite of Julie's arguments, that it was dangerous to marry simply for companionship, affection and reliability. It was dangerous not to, Julie retorted. Settle down sensibly with Toby and be thankful. Why not? You'll regret it if you don't.

I might regret it if I do, Kirsty had maintained. What if I go and fall for someone else?

Now she had.

But she hardly knew him. Couldn't even say if he was married again, had children. No sign of them so far.

'Mushrooms *en croûte*—delicious,' she agreed enthusiastically. 'I go for them.'

'And then the salmon with white wine sauce and scallops, do you think?'

'Perfect. With mange-tout and new potatoes?'

'I agree.' The great grey eyes were looking straight through to his soul, and he knew he'd at last found the woman of his dreams. Kirsty, in her soft pink tracksuit, her blonde hair fastened back with an Indian silk scarf, would hold his heart forever. And luckily she wasn't any sort of dream. She was real.

CHAPTER SIX

RELUCTANTLY, Grant saw Kirsty into her Escort in the car park at St Mark's, watched her drive away, and only then crossed to the side entrance, which was the quickest way up to the children's department. He was walking on air. He was ten feet tall, at least, and life glittered with all the promise there could be.

He found his house physician in a state of scarcely controlled jitters. Quentin had been panicking away quietly to himself since the moment Grant had, in his eyes, abandoned him earlier in the evening. Zoe, the asthmatic girl, didn't seem to Quentin to be half as stable as Grant had alleged. She was still having to struggle for each breath, and although Quentin had put up the drip as Grant had told him to, and he could see from the readings he'd been ordered to take regularly from the Peak Flow Meter that the patient was in fact making progress, however slowly—and the blood-gas levels endorsed this—he had no confidence whatever that the improvement would be maintained while he was there in sole charge. Terrified the patient would suddenly collapse under his eyes, that by himself he'd fail to deal urgently and correctly with any rapid deterioration, he had endured a nail-biting evening. What he would have liked was to have Zoe admitted to Intensive Care, but Grant had vetoed this. They were short of beds, it was Saturday night, notorious for urgent admissions, and they could manage Zoe perfectly well in the ward, no problem. In any case, it would be far less stressing for her with them in the ward.

It was, of course, much more stressing for Quentin—as, in fact, Grant had realised. 'Call me at any time if you're at all worried,' he had said before he left. 'Don't hesitate.'

But Quentin did hesitate. He didn't want, in his very first week in his very first post, to acquire a damning reputation for being alarmist, calling his consultant out for nothing. If only his registrar had been around it would have been so much easier, but she was having the weekend off, and so there was nowhere to go but right up, and that meant Grant. Toby, the senior registrar for the department, was already in the ward, of course, but this didn't help. Quentin found Toby almost as frighteningly senior as Grant, and far more snappish and impatient. In any case, he was fully occupied down at the other end of the ward with Fieldy's house physician, Geraldine, who was as new as Quentin, though apparently far more confident. Of course, if anything awful did happen with Zoe, they would both come running, but this knowledge didn't succeed in boosting Quentin's steadily ebbing confidence.

He'd been overwhelmed with relief earlier when Grant had promised to look in again to check on Zoe before bedtime, and he'd been hanging on to his faltering nerve by his eyelashes, praying for Grant to decide he'd like an early night for once.

Now here he was at last. The mere sight of his tall form with the massive shoulders advancing down the ward reassured Quentin, who went thankfully to meet him.

'No,' Grant agreed placidly, in response to Quentin's agitated bleats, 'I agree she doesn't *look* all that much better yet, and her pulse is still too rapid, as you say. But you've the drip up, that'll have made a difference. Now, tell me. . .' he began, demanding detail. And more detail.

Quentin gabbled anxiously.

'Good. Not bad at all. Let's see what the patient thinks, shall we?' Quentin had met him halfway down the ward, and now Grant led the way to the bedside. 'How are you feeling, Zoe? How's the breathing? Any easier?'

'A tiny bit, perhaps. Only I seem to be getting—awfully tired—well, I always do—so it doesn't seem easier—but I'm better than I was—quite a lot.' The phrases came in jerks between each hard-won breath, and ended with a watery but determined smile. Zoe, though she didn't let on, was as relieved to see Grant as Quentin had been.

'Glad to hear it. Just keep going as you are, and I don't think there'll be any need to use the ventilator.'

'I'd rather—go on breathing for myself—I can do it, I think—I can last out.'

'That's my girl. I think you can, too, so we're agreed, right? You can always rely on what an asthmatic patient tells you, Quentin, remember. No one knows the ins and outs of their condition better than they do themselves.'

Zoe looked immensely cheered, and a bit pleased with herself, too. Even Quentin, though still on edge and taut, was fractionally easier in his mind. Perhaps everything was going to be all right, after all.

Grant put a sudden question. 'Have you eaten?'

Astonished, not sure he'd heard right, Quentin gulped. 'Um—er—eaten?' he squawked. Had he, anyway? What time was it? He'd definitely had lunch—that was long before he'd been called down to Cas to see Zoe, though, and after that, what? It was all a blur.

Grant surveyed him with amusement and some sympathy. Quentin would have been amazed to learn that his consultant knew precisely what he was thinking. 'Supper is the meal I'm referring to, laddie. Have you had supper?'

'Er—no, not actually, I don't think. But it doesn't matter—I can perfectly well——'

'Go down to the canteen now and have it. I'll stay here with Zoe. Take twenty minutes and get a solid meal inside you. Off you go.' He lifted one of his dark brows quizzically. 'I'll be able to manage, you know.'

'Yes, yes, of course, sir. But—but are you sure? I mean, I—I could——'

'Shut up, Quentin, and get out. Stat. And speak to no one except to order your meal. If anyone tries, tell them I'm waiting for you here. As I am. Twenty minutes. From now. Get lost.'

Quentin fled, and Grant sat down in the chair at Zoe's bedside, scrutinised the notes and the lab reports, held up the X-rays against the light and compared them, and listened to the timing and duration of each struggle for breath. Quite soon, simply by his massive presence and tranquil air of calm, he brought her the confidence that was the ultimate boost she needed.

They smiled at one another. 'You're going to come through this bout quite all right, you know,' Grant said in his deep, reassuring voice.

Zoe nodded. 'It's getting easier, I do think.'

'And it'll go on getting easier, remember. That drip's helping you all the time. Don't try to rush at it. Slow and steady does it, remember.' Grant stretched out his long legs with an air of relaxation, which he knew could often be infectious, and deliberately set out to transmit all the signs of a man totally at his ease, taking a quiet half-hour's respite in his own ward.

Tomorrow he'd tell Kirsty about Zoe, he thought. She'd be interested to have an update on the patient he'd been on his way to see when they'd parted. A pity he wasn't going to be able to tell her all about it over breakfast at Long Barn again, but he could hardly summon her to breakfast there two days running, and straight from her bed, too.

Straight from her bed. The ward dissolved, and instead he saw the pink-curtained dormer windows in her bedroom, and had a struggle to push away the next picture—a delightful, beckoning vision of a pink-fleshed Kirsty in her nightdress, warm from sleep, and melting into his encircling arms.

Hey, cool it. This is neither the time nor the place. He focused his eyes on the drip again, and began calculating dosages for the hours ahead. The unsettling view of Kirsty vanished.

He'd see her on Monday, though. Early, even if not at breakfast. On the ward round.

Tonight, he must remember to tell Quentin not on any account to prescribe sedation for Zoe, no matter how much she improved or how tired she was. Unless he told him, Quentin might not realise that sedation could easily lead to a recurrence of the breathing problems.

At this point a rejuvenated Quentin appeared, flushed with food, looking far less harassed, and even slightly jaunty. He'd been away only eighteen minutes, too. Not bad at all.

'Eighteen minutes,' Grant said. 'Well done.'

'And I feel great,' Quentin assured him. 'Thank you very much for that spell, it's very good of you to have stayed on like this.'

Unexpectedly, another figure appeared behind him. Toby Gresham. Grant realised he'd somehow managed to forget Toby's existence.

'Sorry I wasn't available earlier,' he was saying apologetically. 'I've been with the little cystic fibrosis girl in the far bay—we've been having problems there for most of the day, but they told me you were in and had admitted an asthmatic.'

'That's right. Cas rang me, saying you were already tied up in the ward, so I came in.' This was the moment to try to improve his working relationship with Toby, and the competent professional in Grant grabbed the opportunity without hesitation. He embarked on a rapid résumé of the case so far, pressing Quentin to relate Zoe's past history—which he did well, Grant was pleased to find—and encouraging Toby to air his own views at each stage and contribute to a full discussion as to their next moves, and to look at the latest X-ray and lab reports. Grant slipped in his warning to Quentin about no sedation, and outlined the regime he'd planned.

Toby at once offered to oversee it until morning.

'I'll have to stick around with my cystic fibrosis patient for hours yet, and then be on call for her, so I may as well take over this asthmatic too, no problem there. I'd be happy to do it, and you could have the rest of the night off—not that it amounts to a lot, of course. I'm awfully sorry you had to be called out this evening.'

Toby was being very helpful, Grant thought. He'd be silly not to take advantage of his offer, especially as Toby might easily take offence if he was turned down. So he accepted, thanked him, and asked if he'd like a second opinion on the cystic fibrosis girl?

Toby leapt at it, and took him straight along. There could be no doubt about it, he was genuinely concerned about the child, and open to any suggestions from Grant. He was worried, instead of trying to score points and show how brilliant he could be, and grateful for Grant's back-up. He was good with the little girl, and her mother too, humane and caring. This was a different side to him, one Grant had not encountered before.

At one in the morning, Grant left the hospital and drove back to Long Barn. He was stunned. Somehow, over the past twelve hours, he'd managed to overlook Toby's part in Kirsty's life.

His earlier joy evaporated as if it had never been, as he firmly banished any dream of Kirsty and a future with her from his mind, and his heart too. From now on he had to keep himself and his ludicrous yearning for her under strict control. She was not for him. It had all been a mistake.

He was the newcomer in this outfit, he reminded himself. He was the consultant, too, appointed to set up the new service and steer it through its early days, establishing not only stability but a reputation for excellence—or that was what he had planned when he accepted the job. He was not here to upset staff relationships, to interfere in accepted romantic couplings, or to rock the boat in any way whatever. And he certainly must not celebrate his arrival by immediately competing with the senior registrar for Kirsty Holt. More than enough to have snatched the consultant post from him; he mustn't on any account sweep in and grab his girl as well. In any case, he thought miserably, he had no reason to suppose that Kirsty was likely to drop Toby, her companion of so many years, at the mere sight of Grant Sheringham. She had given him no specific encouragement. She had, when he looked back at the day just gone without rose-coloured spectacles, been no more than an agreeable colleague, ready to share a couple of meals and some of her hopes and fears for the service and its patients. Admittedly, she had shared some of her childhood memories, too, and he had told her about his failed marriage, but she had in no way given him a green light to go ahead and make love to her.

To make love to her, he thought flatly. That was what he had seen himself doing. And pretty soon, too. Not for any one-night stand, either. He'd seen a lifetime with the girl of his dreams.

Well, she was the girl of Toby's dreams, too. And Toby had got there first.

All day he'd been deluding himself, Grant knew, believing that a future with Kirsty was opening up in front of him, ready for him to grab it with both hands. He'd been wrong. He had to forget about her, except as a colleague, his partner only in running the new service, not in any other way. He lay awake most of the night arguing with himself, and rose morosely. There was no way out. What he had to do was clear, inescapable. There was no evading it. He must not celebrate his arrival at St Mark's by trying to snatch Toby Gresham's girl.

Hardly surprisingly, on the ward round he was hell on wheels. Curt, snappy, he jumped down everyone's throat on no provocation. Quentin, who'd found him so understanding and supportive on Saturday, and who had been beginning to dare to hope he might actually be going to enjoy his first house job, was savaged when he tried to present the history of Zoe's admission, treatment and present condition. The physiotherapist was eyed disparagingly and subjected to ferocious criticism when she reported on the chest exercises she was planning or had carried out. No one was given any quarter—the nursing staff least of all, and Kirsty was cross-examined frostily whenever she opened her mouth. Even the general practitioner, on the round by special invitation, was interrogated icily, and, contrary to all Grant's instructions to the staff, in no way made to feel at home, or even welcome in the ward.

What on earth had got into him? he asked himself, as he strode away down the corridor, refusing coffee. He had been telling the staff daily that the new service needed all the support it could get from the local doctors, and what had he done? Demolished the unfortunate man.

The day wore on, but nothing changed. Kirsty had her head bitten off yet again, and finally, shattered, retired to her own office and shut the door. What had she ever seen in him? He was horrible. Unkind, impatient, unfair. The worst kind of consultant. Inquisitorial. Supercilious. Uncaring. Arrogant. He was a pain.

Reluctantly, she decided he must be two people. Today's model seemed to have nothing whatever in common with the kind and caring man who had helped her so much—and fed her so superbly—on Saturday.

She hardly knew him, of course. They'd only just met, after all. She'd wildly jumped to a conclusion—or several conclusions, to be honest—about him and decided, on very slight acquaintance, that he was the man of her dreams, when he was still undiscovered country. She'd behaved like a susceptible teenager, falling for broad shoulders on a lean body, dark hair that curled into the nape of his neck, and black eyes that could glint humorously across a dining-table. Grow up, Kirsty Holt.

Yesterday had been a golden dream of happiness. Today was reality. What had occurred was that she had fallen out of love as quickly as she'd so idiotically fallen into it. So much for love, as Julie would tell her straightaway. She should look for tried and trusted companionship, not a blinding flash of lightning to change her world for ever.

Yesterday's dream had been so lovely, though, and she had believed in it implicitly. Stupidly. But today was desolation, and existence stretched uninvitingly ahead of her, grey, bleak and empty.

When Toby stuck his head round the door of her office and invited her to go over the road for a pub lunch at the Lamb, the old coaching inn that now did a thriving trade in meals and snacks for hungry staff from the hospital, she accepted with alacrity. Anything to get out of the department for an hour. Perhaps she'd be able to leave her pain behind in St Mark's and relax into her old life with Toby. Admittedly, her expectations then hadn't been high, but there'd been none of this tearing pain either.

The Lamb did a very good ploughman's, with a choice of Stilton, real Cheddar from Somerset, or unpasteurised Brie, crusty French bread, and a fresh green salad. Both of them enjoyed it, and they had eaten it there together on countless occasions. There was no doubt about it, it was good to be back in this old, safe and companionable existence, and she treated herself to a glass of the Lamb's equally trustworthy Entre-Deux-Mers to mark the return to normality. Toby had a pint of the locally brewed ale that he drank regularly, and raised his glass to her, echoing her own thoughts.

'Great to be on our own again for a while. Somehow I seem hardly to have seen you for days, both of us passing at speed bound for separate meetings, and little else. The new service is certainly going to take up vast tracts of your time, I can see that. By the way, thank you for the terrific meal on Saturday, the venison was out of this world—a shame you weren't there to enjoy it. However, I must say, in your absence, we more than did it justice.'

He gave her what she recognised as a slightly guilty smile. 'It was there for you to eat,' she told him cheerfully. 'And it was hardly your responsibility that I had this problem with the Weybourne family.' More than a little guilty herself, she slid away from the remainder of Saturday evening—she hadn't mentioned the fact that while Toby and Fran had been eating venison at the Old Stables, she'd been eating with Grant at Long Barn. Deceitfully, she realised, she'd simply thanked Toby for looking after Fran that evening. That evening when she'd been out of her tiny, deluded mind with joy. The stab of pain as she remembered threw her momentarily, and she came to as Toby began telling her about the papers he'd heard at the afternoon meeting on Sunday at the Institute of Child Health at Great Ormond Street in central London.

'It was a very good seminar. I was glad I went up for it,' he ended, as they made their way back to St Mark's. 'By the way,' he added, 'you were right about Grant, he's OK. I should have tried to get on with him sooner, and made myself forget that he'd taken the post I was hoping for. Put it behind me, as you said all along. Well, I have now.'

Kirsty tried to feel glad about this. 'Good,' she said faintly, suspecting, only too correctly, that Toby—who always went from one extreme to the other—was about to inform her that Grant Sheringham was the greatest child specialist in the kingdom.

'We worked together on Saturday, on two difficult patients—the asthmatic he'd just admitted, for one, and the little cystic fibrosis girl, Mandy—you remember her. Both of them had breathing difficulties, and I was really worried about Mandy, and thankful for Grant's support. He's a sensible chap, you know, and we got on really well—he has some very interesting ideas,' he added enthusiastically. 'Far more go-ahead than Fieldy. Having him around is going to be really worth while. Useful for the future, too—if I have two consultants behind me for the next job, I mean. I'm not sure it may not have been all for the best, not getting that post, you know.'

'You think so?' Kirsty was secretly amused.

'It may be a better plan not to settle down in Halchester for the remainder of my days, don't you agree?'

Here was a change. 'You feel that?'

'After all, I might get a post in a London teaching hospital, if I just hang on a bit, mightn't I?'

'You never know,' Kirsty said dubiously. She thought he was pushing it a bit to imagine he'd be able to land such a job as his first consultant appointment. Typical Toby, though, she thought affectionately, as they parted on the stairs to the ward. This new plan of his was the direct result of yesterday afternoon's seminar in Great Ormond Street, but she didn't want to throw cold water on his new ideas for his future. Nor could she have said, I told you so about Grant; that would have been a mistake, too, especially as today she was hardly at one with him in finding Grant good to work with.

He was hateful to work with. Firmly, she pushed this reaction away as she went back into her own office to try to shift some of the fast-accumulating paperwork. Forget Grant. He was of no importance whatever. And it was nice to be back on the old familiar footing with Toby again. Old friends were the best. Trusted and true. Dependable.

Her secretary was at lunch, but she'd left a pile of letters on Kirsty's desk to be signed, as well as a sheaf of telephone messages. She waded her way through the letters, and began on the telephone calls.

She should have been in a good mood, she told herself, as she listened to the ringing tone at one of her children's homes. She'd had a super lunch with Toby, and was back on the old terms with him. She enjoyed her new job and its demands. Everything in the garden should have been lovely.

But it wasn't. She was miserable. Anxious, too, as if some doom was waiting round the next corner.

This was ridiculous. She shouldn't have had the glass of wine with her lunch, she decided. That must be what was the matter with her. Wine at midday, that was all. No more, no less.

But the busy, rushed week went on being horrible. It was all because of Grant, she had eventually to admit to herself. It was because he had changed towards her. He was a different man from the one who'd helped her on Saturday morning and then taken her to breakfast. He'd been so sympathetic then, so understanding, and they'd been—or so she'd imagined at the time—close. Truly close. They had seemed, then, to have a natural affinity.

She'd been jumping the gun, of course, when she'd so crazily believed they were only the tiniest step away from recognising that they were made for each other. But she'd genuinely supposed, God help her, that she'd fallen in love with the man of her dreams.

How wrong could you be?

All week, of course, they worked together. On ward rounds, at the bedside, at case conferences, in patients' homes, or sometimes in her office with parents.

It wasn't that Grant was in the least unpleasant. After that one day—which the staff labelled Black Monday, and never forgot—he had returned to his former brisk efficiency. True, he didn't waste time on small-talk, but that had never been his habit. The trouble was more that he didn't waste any time whatever anywhere in her vicinity. He never lingered. Often, too, after the ward round, say, he'd turn abruptly on his heel and be gone, when they'd been expecting a pause, a quick chat session, and a cup of tea or coffee with a biscuit or two. Instead he'd shoot off at speed, leaving Quentin to sort out with the remainder of the team the details about the cases they'd seen.

It was as if he couldn't stand being near her. She must surely be imagining this, and yet she knew she wasn't. She faced it, and pain engulfed her. She spoke sternly to herself, denying what she secretly knew was happening. Don't exaggerate, she told herself. Grant was simply busy, like everyone else, and he hadn't yet been in the post for a month, even, so there were constant demands for decisions and agreement from colleagues and staff who didn't yet know him well enough to read his mind, who were not familiar with his attitudes and decisions.

There could be nothing personal in it, Kirsty informed herself a dozen times a day. She was hardly the centre of his universe; he was almost certainly unconscious of whether she was around or not. Don't read hidden meaning into the departures of a hard-driven consultant getting through his day at a driving pace.

But it was all so different from that brilliant Friday and Saturday, when she had felt the world had changed for ever because he was in it. And it hurt.

There was no communication between them now. There was *nothing* between them. Zilch. Nil. Zero. She must have invented the theory that there had been anything at all out of the ordinary in their relationship. It must have been merely a figment of her imagination. Over-excited, that's what she'd been, on a high at the culmination of her hopes for the new service and her new post, and the meeting and then the party that evening had gone to her head. Now she had to pull herself together and get on with the job, instead of yearning after Grant like some besotted teenager. Accept him for what he undoubtedly was, the highly competent director of the new service. Her partner in this, if nothing else.

But she couldn't bear the distance yawning between them, and as each day went stolidly by, and a second week followed the first, she felt increasingly estranged from him, and minded it more and more. Far from finding herself used to it, misery settled on her like a heavy blanket. She wanted to forget about him, not to care, but however hard she fought, whenever she encountered him—in the ward, in the office, merely walking along a corridor or coming out of the lift as she entered it—her heart insisted on lifting, and a mad thrill surged through her.

Her stupid heart had to learn better. There was nothing so special about Grant, she reminded it forcefully. But it didn't make any difference. Her heart continued to lift as soon as he appeared.

They had planned to do a round together of their in-patients at least every other day, though with so many outside visits to make it was a problem, especially as every Wednesday there was the big round in the main ward, with both consultants, Fieldy and Grant, making decisions as to who could be nursed at home, who could be transferred to the upstairs ward in preparation for going home, while their mothers or fathers learnt how to manage them under supervision. This round was attended by almost everyone from the department—Toby, two registrars, both house physicians, Emma and Dinah as well as Kirsty, not to mention physios, occupational therapists—who were involved in seeing if homes could be adapted to suit patient care—and social workers. Quite often, too, several general practitioners were there, ready to discuss the management of their patients in their own homes. Grant was particularly keen that these family doctors should not only feel welcome, but also know they were being listened to—after all, they had the continuing care of these children, year after year, while admission to St Mark's was often a comparatively brief incident. It was vital, Grant had stressed to Kirsty, that both she and Dinah should always attend the big round, since this was when decisions were reached, along with parents and family doctors, as to who could go home for treatment there, and how soon they could be ready to leave.

'I'm entirely easy, though,' he told her crisply, 'As to whether it's you or Dinah on the round in our own ward upstairs.'

What he said was both sensible and practical, no doubt about it, but just the same, she felt snubbed, and hurt, too, no matter how ridiculous she knew this to be. She was interchangeable with Dinah, he didn't care which of them was there—very likely he hardly knew the difference. Just nursing staff to him.

In fact, it was Dinah who told her that Verity Blakelock was back with them, in the ward with another bout of rheumatic fever.

'Oh, wouldn't you know? I *am* sorry. When did she come in?'

'Yesterday evening. Her mother rang for an ambulance, and she was taken to Casualty. In Cas they rang for a paediatrician fast, and luckily Toby was still in the department. He remembered her at once, so he went down to see her. Obviously she had to be admitted, but he thought better if she came straight into one of our beds, in the circs, and he rang Grant, who agreed, so here she is, with us again.'

'Only what we expected, of course—or I suppose you could say slightly better than we expected, in that at least she's back here, and we know her latest history. She could have been still undiagnosed in some hospital the other side of the country.'

'That's true. Verity told me their caravan is back in the campsite up on the cliffs where they were before. Apparently the owner told them at the beginning of the summer that they could come back and park there free again once the season was over. I thought I'd drop in on mum while I'm on my calls today, and see if I can get any sense out of her.'

'Good idea—though I bet you won't. She's dippy as they come. But you might find out where they've been since we last saw them—moving around or in one place. Not that I truly expect it to make any difference. I'll bet you anything that nitwitted Perdita never took Verity anywhere for her monthly medication, in spite of the fact that both Fieldy and

I, separately and together, spent hours telling her how important it was for Verity's future well-being that they kept up with the prophylaxis.'

'I don't really remember the mother. I only met her for the ten days or so we had Verity in the ward, before she went to you out at Northcliffe. I must say, the general impression left with me was that she was a total drop-out, and probably stoned half the day.' Dinah had never had much time for either the failures or the eccentrics of this world.

'Verity herself understood perfectly well about her medication, and she would have remembered to see about it, I'm sure, if they'd been anywhere near a doctor—we gave her a prescription and a covering letter. But I'd be surprised if that useless Perdita paid any attention. Verity has a heart murmur already, Fieldy said—he's convinced that she's had more than one bout of rheumatic fever in the past, before she landed on us, though neither of them will admit to it, nor to any previous hospital admissions, so we were never able to track down any past history from anywhere. I'm sure they're covering up, though, both of them, simply because they've been through it all before, and been told how important it is for Verity to have regular medication to try to prevent recurrence of the infection. Each time she has a bout, she's running an almost certain risk of worsening her heart condition. Fieldy said, the way they're going on, if we're right—and I feel sure we are—Verity'll be needing heart surgery when she's still in her early twenties.'

'You'd think even that silly mother would be able to take that much on board, and be frightened for Verity.' Dinah was caustic.

'She lives for the moment, if you ask me, and doesn't do much worrying about things that may never happen. Just looks the other way.' Kirsty thought of Annabel—and Fran, too, for that matter. Neither of them was what anyone could call far-sighted, and certainly they were both experts in dodging anything they didn't like.

'New Age travellers,' Dinah said scathingly. 'Stone Age, more like.'

'Yes, if ever anyone needed a proper roof over her head, with proper heating and adequate hygiene, it's that poor chick Verity. It might make all the difference. The social workers actually found them accommodation, back in the spring when it's really difficult, all credit to them, but Perdita wouldn't hear of it. Devoted to that beastly caravan and wandering free, as she calls it. Oh, well, I wish you joy of her this afternoon.'

'Gee, thanks. If I find I'm getting nowhere—only too likely—I'll call you in.'

Kirsty sighed. 'I just wish I'd been able to think up something, anything at all, that we could do to see that Verity had proper treatment and somewhere to live that doesn't damage her further. Some hope.' A sudden urgent need to talk to Grant about Verity possessed her. She longed to be able to confide her anxiety and distress about the likely outcome for this ten-year-old unless they could succeed in getting through to her wacky mother, make her comprehend the immense importance of continuing Verity's medication all the year round. She needed a proper roof over her head, too. Perhaps Grant would succeed where she had failed—perhaps it might turn out that Perdita was putty in his hands, would do whatever he told her without demur.

Who was she kidding? Only herself, Kirsty decided ruefully. Luckily, she was so busy that, in spite of her misery, the days rushed by.

This meant, of course, that she hardly saw Fran from one day to the next. Luckily, though, she appeared to be happily occupied in and around Halchester. She was unforthcoming, if not downright evasive, as to how she actually spent her waking hours, but then, Fran had always been vague about what she was doing—often exceedingly little—and never failed to rebuff any enquiries. She'd met masses of people at the party the evening she'd arrived, she told Kirsty, and they had introduced her to other people, natch. Then, on the Saturday when Toby had taken her to lunch, they'd been to the Lamb, and she'd met a huge number more from the hospital, and one thing led to another, didn't it?

With Fran, of course, as Kirsty had recognised years ago, it always did, and pretty smartly, at that.

Their own encounters in the past couple of weeks consisted, for the most part, in Kirsty rushing in as Fran rushed out, or vice versa. However, one evening when they both managed to be inside the Old Stables together, Kirsty persuaded Fran to go across to see Mrs Anstruther with her. The old lady always appreciated a new face, and in any case, she had promised to introduce Fran to their landlady.

Mrs Anstruther, typically, at once offered them sherry, but Fran—who loathed the drink—turned it down immediately, but with such charm that Mr Anstruther was enchanted with her, and produced the tonic with ice and lemon that she wanted instead with approbation, obviously considering her young guest delightfully innocent and inexperienced. Nothing could have been further from the truth, but Fran, as Kirsty knew only too well, always threw herself whole-heartedly into whatever role was expected. The three of them sat in the conservatory watching the sunset, but then Kirsty said regretfully that she would have to go and see to their meal.

'Oh, I should come with you and do something to help,' Fran exclaimed, to Kirsty's secret amusement. Fran had never done more in any kitchen than drape herself against the nearest counter-top or dresser and feast on tastes of whatever was available. 'But it's so simply gorgeous here watching the sky that I can't bear to leave so soon. Am I being the most frightful nuisance to you? Can you possibly put up with me for another five minutes, do you think?' She fluttered her eyelashes and looked so meltingly at Mrs Anstruther that the normally indomitable old lady melted too.

'My dear, there's nothing I'd like better,' she said at once. 'I'd love Kirsty to stay on too, if she could, but I know how busy she is, and. . . It's all right, Kirsty, I'm not trying to press you. You go back to the Old Stables, and I'll send this captivating young sister of yours across in, say, half an hour. Would that be all right? You could spare an old woman that long? Five minutes is far too short.'

'Half an hour would be fine,' Kirsty agreed. 'And thanks so much for my sherry.' She took herself back to the Old Stables a little uncomfortably. She hadn't enjoyed seeing her dear old landlady manipulated quite so blatantly by her conscienceless sister, and she felt like shaking Fran and ordering her straight home and no nonsense.

She was wrong, she realised, as she let herself in. Mrs Anstruther was enjoying every second of Fran's company, which was giving her a boost.

What was more, she realised, she herself was getting a boost from being alone and undisturbed in the Old Stables for a while. She'd forgotten how many problems living under the same roof as Fran always posed. It was more than a bit of a strain, she admitted unwillingly to herself, with this new job in its very first weeks, to have to remember to cater for Fran, and to return home tired out to an untidy house and a kitchen cluttered with dirty pans and used dishes—like now. She had to load the dishwasher before she could start the meal. She was sick and tired, too, of the house resounding to the pop music Fran liked on full blast, fed up with finding her bedroom a shambles yet again, and of being woken in the small hours by Fran crashing about downstairs with unknown males, seeing them off noisily, and then thumping about, running a bath and playing her radio while she had it.

She must be getting old and set in her ways. Her attitude was ridiculous. She'd looked forward to having Fran with her, and now she was simply being crabby and disagreeable, fed up at St Mark's, and fed up at home. She was antisocial and horrid, and none of it was poor Fran's fault at all. What it must be was that for years she'd never been with Fran except when she was on holiday, whereas now she was busy and a bit stressed, and only saw Fran at the end of the day when she'd already had enough. Guiltily, she set out to make her a truly delicious meal. Lamb chops with redcurrant jelly? No, Fran would think that conventional and dull. Lamb with ratatouille would be more like it, and she had both in the freezer. She took them out and put them to defrost, while she thought about potato, rice or pasta to go with them. Baked potato with *fromage frais* and chives would be nice. . . No, on second thoughts, while Fran was sophisticated on the surface, food-wise she remained, secretly, a chips with everything teenager. Chips, then.

A good three-quarters of an hour later Fran came bursting into the house. 'I must be dreadfully late, I am so fearfully sorry, I simply couldn't get away from the old trout. Have I ruined your meal?'

'Not in the least. I gave you quarter of an hour extra in my mind, I was fairly certain you'd need it—after all, I know you, and Mrs Anstruther too. But the food's about ready now. If I dish up straight away, are you ready to eat?'

'Absolutely,' Fran assured her, racing upstairs. Twenty minutes later, she floated down in an entirely new outfit, freshly made up and smelling of Kirsty's Chanel. 'Gosh, have you been waiting?' she exclaimed, at sight of Kirsty on the sofa with her legs up, reading the paper. 'I thought you were going to dish up?'

'I have. It's waiting in the microwave—sit down and I'll bring it through.' Kirsty had plated the meal ready to eat, and she switched on the microwave, poured herself Perrier and asked Fran what she'd like to drink.

'Nothing, thanks. I'm already bursting with tonic, and I'm going to the Lamb to meet some people between eight and nine, so I'll have a drink then in any case. And there's a disco to go on to, so I'll be late. Don't wait up, will you? However——' she paused dramatically, her fork piled with lamb and ratatouille '—this is the last time, I promise you, that I'll disturb you in the middle of the night. Absolutely the last time.' Her eyes gleamed as she stared across the table at her sister. 'Guess what?'

She looked extremely pleased with herself, and Kirsty wondered if she'd extracted an air fare from their father and was off to join her mother in California the next morning after breakfast. 'I've not the faintest idea,' she said truthfully. 'You can't be going to spend every evening in and go to bed at nine. I give up. Tell.'

'Mrs Anstruther has offered me a room for as long as I need it. Isn't that great? She asked me how we were managing, the two of us in this tiny cottage, and so I told her it was jolly hard on you, in fact, so she said straight away that there were plenty of empty rooms there, and I'd be doing her a favour if I used one of them. So what do you think of that?'

Kirsty could have thumped her sister. Fran had been up to her tricks again, manipulating Mrs Anstruther. From the moment she'd asked if she could stay on and watch the sky for another five minutes, Fran had been planning to move into the big old house. Incorrigible.

On the other hand, Kirsty had to admit, whatever Fran's motives, Mrs Anstruther would genuinely enjoy having a young creature like Fran in and out of the house, and her daughter would be thankful to hear there would be someone under the same roof—even if the someone was as scatty as Fran. By simply being on the spot every night, Fran would be an insurance policy. Kirsty's thoughts circled uneasily.

'After all,' Fran added sympathetically, 'you must have been going mad, with me underfoot non-stop.'

'Hardly non-stop,' Kirsty pointed out. 'In actual fact, except for the hours of darkness, one of us is nearly always out. You will go gently with Mrs Anstruther, won't you, love? Try not to crash around at midnight, or anything like that? She is in her late eighties, remember.'

'Wow, is she really? That's a huge age, isn't it? Of course, I could see she was old, but I never imagined that old. She's quite a sweetie, though, isn't she? You don't need to worry, I won't do a thing to upset her. I'll be like a mouse creeping in and out, I promise.'

Fat chance. At this improbable scenario, Kirsty had to grin, despite her many misgivings. 'Just don't bang doors or play the radio loudly in the small hours, will you? Did you—um—did you offer her any rent or anything like that?' Before the words were out of her mouth, she knew what the answer had to be.

'*Rent*?' Fran repeated, rather as if the word were a hideous obscenity. 'How could I possibly do that?'

'I don't quite know,' Kirsty admitted. 'But I do think we ought to try, even if we know for certain she's not going to accept. And perhaps you might take her in some flowers tomorrow? The shop nearly opposite St Mark's, down the road from the Lamb, is perfectly reliable, and not fearfully expensive either.'

'OK, will do. Not to worry.' Fran crammed the last of the chips into her mouth. 'That was a super meal, you are an angel. And now I must fly. See you in the morning, and no need to panic, I'll go gently with the old dear, truly I will.'

Outside gravel crunched, and a car hooted.

Fran leapt to her feet, grabbed her sling-bag and her fluffy mohair shawl, and fled.

CHAPTER SEVEN

LIKE most hospitals, St Mark's had always been a hotbed of gossip, and the rumours were flying, the grapevine buzzing, as staff compared notes busily and exchanged news of the latest sightings. Routinely, everyone knew which couples had met up in the Lamb, what they had said to one another, and where they had gone afterwards—out for a meal, to a film, to sail, play tennis or go to the disco. Or, of course, simply into a car together and away. Hardly, then, to share a grammar and polish up their French, though that had been the serious assertion of one couple under scrutiny. As it happened, it had been the truth, though no one had ever believed it.

No one, in any case, supposed Toby Gresham and Fran Holt to be studying French or any other language. It was obvious to the dimmest brain that all they were interested in was each other.

The one person who knew nothing about this, the hospital was agreed, was Kirsty Holt, and her friends and supporters were out of their minds with anxiety and panic, not to mention rage.

'You can't possibly tell her,' Emma argued over coffee in the ward office with Dinah, the door for once firmly shut.

'She's sure going to find out if I don't get in first,' Dinah pointed out. 'And it would be much worse for her to discover it out of the blue here on the ward, or something like that.'

'It's going to be ghastly for her in any case. Losing Toby after all these years, and to her own sister, too.'

'That rat Toby.' Dinah ground her teeth and glared across the desk.

Dinah was the one who swung into action at any crisis, and Emma eyed her uneasily. 'You mustn't tell her, Di,' she said urgently. 'It'd be——'

The door opened, and Kirsty came in. 'Ah, you're both here,' she said, pleased. 'I've caught you together. That's nice, and it'll save a bit of time, too. What I wanted to talk about is the Weybourne family.'

'I know,' Dinah said flatly. 'What on earth are we going to do about that set-up?' But she looked away, not meeting Kirsty's eyes.

What on earth could be up with Dinah? Kirsty wondered. She was never evasive. On the contrary, if anything, almost too straightforward and honest, and given to blurting out things that were far better left unsaid. Well, whatever it was, it would have to wait. Time was short, and they had to talk about the Weybournes; that was the immediate problem.

Linda was still in the ward. Nearly three weeks had gone by since her admission, the entire family had quite recovered from their colds, and Jill was longing to have her back home again, she said, but Linda kept finding a reason to postpone the move.. Infuriatingly, she succeeded in producing some new reason for not leaving St Mark's before any plans could be finalised. Subject always to recurrent infections—it was one of the hazards of her condition—

she blew up a temperature with maddening regularity, and they had to keep her in yet again for investigation.

'The crux of the problem is to find out what Linda really wants, and whether she can have it,' Kirsty said.

'Of course, Jill Weybourne is saying "I told you so" loud and clear,' Dinah commented. 'She's sticking now to what she said that evening you and I brought Linda back in. It's all our doing, we let her get away with it then, and so now she's playing us up.'

'From the long-term point of view, she may be right,' Kirsty admitted. 'I've thought about it a lot, and asked myself again and again, but I still don't think we either could or should have done anything else that evening. Anyway, right or wrong, it doesn't fully explain why Linda wants to stay here now. I know we agreed then that she may have been going through the inevitable post-honeymoon stage of living at home——' at the words 'post-honeymoon' Dinah undoubtedly winced, and dodged Kirsty's eyes again, so that she was alerted. Was that what was wrong with Dinah? Was her love-life in ruins? She'd better ask around, Kirsty decided, find out what was going on. Not now, though '—but we were fairly certain she'd work her way through it successfully. Linda's always been a determined fighter, no matter what.'

'Jill thinks that's why we shouldn't have taken her in. She says Linda would have struggled on if we'd left her where she was, but now she's had a taste of back in hospital, she likes it, and she's opting out of trying at home.'

'Well, if so, oughtn't we to listen to her? Jill doesn't necessarily know best always. Children have rights too, and Linda's a very adult thirteen, poor sweet. Her existence is incredibly hard and exhausting, just keeping going day after day, and she's the one who knows what it feels like to be wheelchair-bound at the best and almost totally paralysed. If she wants a break in hospital, why shouldn't she have it?'

'Fieldy would be with you there, I rather think,' Emma put in. 'He and Grant came back and saw her together after the big round the other day, and Fieldy said not to worry, Linda was the best judge of what she needed. He told Grant he'd be inclined to allow whatever it is to take its natural course. As a matter of fact, Fieldy, bless him—not much misses him, does it?—came up with an off-beat suggestion. He thinks Linda may have been a bit lonely at home, after all the companionship she's been used to.'

'Lonely?' This was indeed a new idea, and one that had not occurred to Kirsty. 'But surely, with her parents and two sisters, and the volunteers in every day——'

'Ah, but Jill stopped most of the volunteers after the early days, didn't she?' Dinah interrupted. 'Gradually, but steadily, she took on more and more herself. There's no night nurse now. Jill and Kevin take it in turns to get up during the night, and Jill baths Linda, too, with one of the other children to help. She deals with most of the nursing care, too—the district nurse only goes in once a week to check, these days, and I go in once a week, too. So, apart from the two volunteers who get her up and dressed, while Jill is getting the other two off to school, Linda can't actually be seeing anyone other than her family most days—after all, the plan for her to go to the comprehensive with her sisters fell through, remember?'

'Yes, I jolly well do.' Even the memory of this incensed Kirsty. 'I was livid at the time. I think it was outrageous. The wretched teacher refused to take the responsibility. She does have a tutor most days, though, doesn't she? That hasn't fallen apart, has it?'

'No, but that's only one extra person, and an adult, at that. Her sisters are away at school all day, so there'd just be Jill and the tutor.'

Kirsty nodded. 'And she'd been used to the ward, with hordes of kids, and faces changing all the time, too. That's right. What's more, she used to go across to the asthmatics' school whenever she was fit enough. I think, you know, Fieldy may be on to something—and not for the first time.'

'What would we do without him?' Emma added.

'This needs thinking out, doesn't it?' Kirsty asked. 'Jill's idea may be mistaken—or, come to think of it, it could be half the story. What if Jill, super as she is in so many ways, has become possessive, and—and a bit sort of smothering, and is incidentally cutting Linda off even more from people?'

'It could happen. In fact, I think you may have hit on it, you and Fieldy between you,' Dinah agreed.

'I must make time and have a long talk with Linda,' Kirsty said. 'By the way, Di, have you talked to Kevin lately? Do we know what he thinks?'

'No, he's at work all day. I've just seen Jill when she visits. 'Are you thinking——'

'I don't know quite what I'm thinking, to be

honest. It's just I suddenly wondered, maybe there's an extra strand, too. That evening we admitted Linda, I got a strong impression there was something on the go between Linda and her father that I couldn't put my finger on. She adores him, of course, but quite what part that plays in the whole situation, I can't see. Not at present.'

'He sure was set on her coming back in, that evening,' Dinah recollected. 'No doubt about that. Do you suppose we could be wrong about her being lonely after all, and it's simply that she thinks her father doesn't want her back at home, thinks looking after her is too much for her mother, and so she's trying to please him by staying here as long as possible?'

'That's yet another possibility,' Kirsty agreed. 'Who comes to visit her?' she asked Emma.

'Jill comes nearly every afternoon, as she's always done, but I don't know about the evenings. That's when Kevin used to come, but I'd have to ask the late staff.' She made a quick note. 'That's quite an idea, I do think. What if Kevin's encouraging her to stay put, to take the load off Jill?'

'Not only take the load off,' Kirsty commented. 'Maybe it's the old, familiar story, only the other way round from what Jill was telling us. Maybe Kevin would like a bit more attention and a bit less hard work at home. Perhaps he's the one who'd like to go back to the old regime, with Linda safely in hospital being visited.'

Emma nodded. 'Families are complicated,' she said. 'And some of that has to be true, even if only unconsciously—none of them may recognise what they're actually up to.'

'What I need is a good long talk with Kevin, it seems to me, as well as Linda—I'll look in one evening and have a chat with him on his own. I can sound him out on the other theory, too—that she may be bored and lonely tucked away at home.'

Dinah leapt in immediately. 'You're meant to be working days, remember? Unless I call you out for an emergency. This isn't any sort of emergency.'

'No, but it's nothing. Wouldn't take me more than half an hour or so, and it might tell us what we need to know.'

Dinah snorted derisively. 'Half an hour talking to Kevin—only it's more likely to be an hour—another half-hour, I bet, talking to Linda herself, ten minutes with someone who catches you on the way out for a word about whatever, plus a ten-minute drive each way, and you've spent two hours of your evening, before you know it. Kirsty, you simply can't work all the hours God gives.' No wonder, she was thinking, Toby's found other company to fill in his evenings.

'Only one evening, Di. That's hardly going to cause me to collapse from overwork, is it? I'll see him one evening soon, that's definite, and have a good talk to Linda, too.'

'OK, so I'm talking to myself,' Dinah said sarcastically. 'I know when I'm beaten. Go your own way and take the consequences.'

Emma was increasingly uneasy. Dinah in this mood might come out with anything. Hastily she butted in herself. 'I think what we're going to need for the Weybournes is a hospital case conference. Put all our heads together. Hospital, though, not district. No social workers.'

'Good plan,' Kirsty agreed. 'Could you lay it on,

once I've seen Kev and talked it through with him?'

'Just give me the word.'

'Thanks. On my way, then—oh, I forgot. I'm going to see the Nicholsons this afternoon—anything more you want to say about Zoe?'

'Not really. I think we covered it fairly thoroughly the other day. The GP's still maintaining—but he's a terrible old worry-guts, as I told you—that we made a big mistake in deciding Zoe could live at home and go to school locally, instead of finding her a place in another residential school when Northcliffe closed. But Grant thinks what we're seeing may be no more than just a settling-in period, while she gets used to the new school plus living at home. I tend to agree with that, but he wanted you to see her as well, and her mother, if possible separately.'

'Yes, he told me.' One of the conversations she treasured, held, as so often, in a corridor, at speed. A shaft of brilliant light in her day, just the same. 'I'm planning to get there early, before Zoe comes back from school, so that I can have a talk with Mrs Nicholson without Zoe on the premises.'

Dinah gave a short laugh. 'Mrs N is quite something,' she commented. 'You'll see.' She raised her eyes heaven-wards.

'Oh, lord. Well, this time I'm really off—see you,' Kirsty said, and left the room. Preoccupied with the Weybournes, the Nicholsons, what Grant had said about Zoe, and the other families on her list she had to fit in, she quite forgot she'd been bothered earlier by Dinah's attitude, or that she'd begun to suspect she might be having problems in her love-life. She was certainly far too busy herself to think at all about Toby or Fran, and even Grant was hardly in her thoughts until she ran into him crossing the car park.

'Hello,' she said automatically. 'Lovely day. Windy, though.' She had no idea that she spoke in the chilliest of tones as she passed on her way.

His response could hardly be called warm. 'Quite so,' he snapped as he strode past, not so much as the hint of a smile touching his lips. Nothing gave the remotest clue that his inner eye would hoard this momentary glimpse of Kirsty—stepping blithely, as he saw it, across the car park in tawny autumnal tweeds, her shining hair swept into a golden plait down her back that he yearned to get his hands on and undo.

A familiar desolation possessed Kirsty as he disappeared, even though she tried to deny its existence, concentrating instead on checking her street map for the Nicholson address. Her thoughts determinedly anchored to Halchester geography and the ups and downs of Zoe's asthma, she did her best to block out her own underlying pain.

Dinah had mentioned that the Nicholsons' house was dreamy, saying she saw why Zoe wanted so much to live at home, but even so, Kirsty was taken aback. Set in an early Victorian terrace climbing the hill behind the cathedral, it turned out to be a small period gem. Its stucco frontage had been painted magnolia, the square-paned lattice windows picked out in white, there was a graceful fanlight over a black front door, and black wrought-iron balconies at every window. Every inch of it gleamed with paint and polish, while the balconies cascaded with pink geraniums flourishing in the October sun. Tubs on either side of the front door cascaded too, as did hanging baskets on either side of the porch. She pressed the bell, heard chimes sounding, and then quick footsteps.

Mrs Nicholson, dressed as if for a cocktail party—could this simply be her normal afternoon attire?—opened the door and welcomed Kirsty into a hall almost the opposite of what, after seeing the pretty, decorative frontage, she had expected. The hall was bare and almost empty, except for a dark oak chest with a plain oval mirror above it, a straight-backed oak chair either side; the flooring consisted of large grey and white tiles, while the staircase had been stripped and polished, and was carpetless.

Mrs Nicholson, in her flowery suit, her hair permed, rinsed and carefully set, her make-up flawless, undoubtedly matched the front of her house, but not this hall. It was, of course, a hall for an asthmatic, dust- and pollen-free. Had Mrs Nicholson done violence to her home-making instincts for the sake of her daughter? If so, did she resent it?

'I suppose,' Kirsty began, following her instinct, 'you can't have flowers indoors because of Zoe. But outside, you have the most wonderful display.'

She made contact instantly.

'Oh, you're so right,' Zoe's mother exclaimed. 'I used to have a house absolutely filled with flowers, but now Zoe's here at home we simply dare not have any, so I have rather let myself go outside, I'm afraid. My husband says I've overdone it.'

'They're gorgeous,' Kirsty assured her. 'I was standing outside admiring them before I rang your bell.'

Mrs Nicholson, clearly pleased, led the way into

a sitting-room that ran the full length of the house, with windows at either end. Light and airy, its style was in the same idiom as that of the hall, though here the floor was parquet. There were plain white roller blinds at the tall sash windows, terracotta-coloured walls, and a number of Scandinavian-type couches and chairs with pale wooden arms and tawny leather thonging.

'We did the entire house over when we knew Zoe was going to be living at home—previously, you see, she was never here for more than a few days at the beginning and end of term. We always took her to Switzerland for Christmas, skiing, and in the spring and summer holidays we stayed in the mountains, too, and my husband used to fly out as often as he could. Zoe was so much better in the mountain air, it was a joy to see her so well.'

'The house looks lovely, but it must have been a difficult decision, to change your home completely.' Kirsty was asking herself if the atmosphere of strain around Zoe was connected with this.

'It's quite different from what it used to be. I originally had chintz and bowls of flowers everywhere, and fitted carpets. Actually, making it over has been enormous fun, I must say. Nothing like a few changes to buck one up.' Mrs Nicholson's eyes twinkled, and she suddenly produced a warm, humorous grin at odds with her stiff and formal exterior. 'It's so lovely having a daughter at home, I can't tell you how much I'm enjoying myself. Zoe says she's going to get me into jeans and sweatshirts soon—*me*, I ask you? I haven't been so alive since we were first married.'

Kirsty did her best to imagine Mrs Nicholson out

of her chintzy suit and high heels and into jeans and a sweatshirt, but her imagination balked.

'All my cooking has changed, too,' Mrs Nicholson went on, 'because of watching Zoe's allergies. In fact, my daily routine has altered completely now Zoe's home. I just pray we can keep going, that what we've done will be enough, and that her health doesn't break down. Having her here with us is a huge responsibility. Huge. We have to do our very best for her, but underneath, I'm so dreadfully worried that we may fail her—she's so fantastically keen to pull this off and live at home like an ordinary girl, go to the grammar school and take her O levels and then her As. It's up to me to see I don't let her down—if her health doesn't stand up to it, it'll be my fault.'

So there was the explanation, one that none of them had suspected. Not resentful parents at all, but loving and over-protective.

'We thought we were giving her the earth, all these holidays abroad—and in the early days they were difficult to afford—but now it turns out that all she longs to do is live here in Halchester and be like everyone else. I don't know how I'll be able to bear it for her if it doesn't work, and yet I have this ghastly feeling it's not going to. Dr Hardcastle doesn't think it will, you know, he's always been dead against it.' Mrs Nicholson's hands were twisting against her fashionable skirt, and she looked anguished.

So this was the problem confronting Zoe, Kirsty thought. Loving, anxious parents foreseeing disaster, and worry-gutting Dr Hardcastle, who hadn't wanted Zoe to come home in the first place and, now she was here, had rushed her into hospital as soon as he was called out to see her.

This diagnosis was confirmed by Zoe herself, when she returned from school and they both went to her room for Kirsty to take her blood-pressure and measure her breathing.

'I'm perfectly all right, if only they'd stop fussing,' Zoe insisted. 'I've got my nebuliser always, I know exactly when to use it, and if they'd just keep out of the way I'm sure I could cope. But they're not used to me wheezing, you see, and they panic like mad, which of course doesn't help one bit. However hard I try to manage, I get worse while they stand over me—well, it's *because* I'm trying so hard, instead of relaxing, that I get worse.'

'Yes, I can see just what you mean.'

'At school it used to be so easy—no one took much notice, everyone used their nebulisers, the staff took it for granted. They did watch us fairly carefully, I suppose, they must have done, but you never noticed them doing it. Anyway, they never cared so dreadfully—Mum and Dad are practically jumping up and down, they're so frightened they've done the wrong thing by letting me come home to live, and Dr Hardcastle's as bad as they are. Worse. He makes me lose what confidence I've got left, and I get worse as soon as he appears with his long face. He's doom-laden, that's what he is. Not a bit like Dr Sheringham. When he was looking after me in the ward, the moment he appeared, I was sure I was going to be OK.'

'I know what you mean,' Kirsty said with feeling.

'He sat by me the first evening—it was quite late, he'd sent the other doctor to get himself some supper, and he just sat by me quietly. Simply having him there made everything all right. I stopped worrying, and I was able to relax at last, and get a breathing rhythm going again. I should never have let myself get worked up that day—there really wouldn't have been the slightest need for me to come into hospital. I would have been OK if they'd just left me alone to get on with it by myself. But no, they had to ring Dr Hardcastle, and all he wanted was to put me in hospital, get me off his hands, because he was just as frightened as they were. So the next thing was that I got frightened too, because it was all going wrong, and there didn't seem to be anything I could do to stop everything going right out of control—and then I truly couldn't get my breath any more, so it was panic stations all round, and there I was in Casualty, getting worse and worse, and not able to stop myself.'

'I do exactly see how it was,' Kirsty told her. 'Another time, you can just get your parents to ring the home-care service, and one of us—me, or Dinah, or Dr Sheringham, if you need him—will come straight away. We'll either take you in, or we'll stay here with you while you cope.'

'Oh, if I could be sure that would work!' Zoe exclaimed poignantly. 'If only they'd didn't mind so terribly—they feel they've failed all round if I get so much as the hint of a wheeze. And I'm bound to, I do on and off, and it doesn't mean a thing. But they instantly decide they've not been looking after me properly, or I wouldn't have it. They've made the wrong decision, they should never have let me live at home, they're ruining my life. It's all their fault. The trouble is, I do matter so much to them. If only I wasn't so precious, and they could stop bothering about me so much—that's what's so different from living at school, of course, and that's what I simply hadn't allowed for. At school everyone had asthma, and we all had to manage it as well as we could. It was a perfectly ordinary thing, it was taken for granted, no one got excited about it. It was no big deal. Here, it's life and death. I feel Mum and Dad are there counting my every breath—they think I might die at any moment and it'll be their fault.'

Growing up was not easy, not for anyone, not for parent or child, Kirsty reflected, as she drove slowly through the rush-hour across Halchester and at last along the cliff road. When she saw, time after time, the problems sick children faced daily, routinely, whether in their own homes or in hospital, she felt ashamed of supposing, as she had too often done, that her own upbringing had been in anyway hard. All right, so she couldn't remember her mother, but Cathy had been all the mum that any child could need. And what if Cathy hadn't been around throughout her childhood? She'd never lost touch with her, and Fran's mother Annabel, while far from perfect, had been generous and well-meaning, even if blindingly self-centred and, like Fran, scatty and thoughtless, too. There was nothing whatever wrong with her father, either, except that he was too often absent. She had had it easy.

She passed Highcliffe, and drove on up to the campsite at the very top of Cliffside Drive. Before she went home, she wanted to catch Perdita Blakelock, if she could. She hadn't been to visit Verity for four days now, and a little encouragement to drop in at the hospital would do no harm.

She could see the Blakelock caravan, parked just past the camp office and the showers. She could see two figures as well, moving around, going in and out of the van, apparently tidying up and doing some clearing. It seemed most unlike Perdita to be so energetic, but perhaps the owner of the campsite had insisted. Kirsty prayed that he wasn't about to evict them.

She locked the car and went to find out what was going on. Perdita was looking more beautiful than ever, she thought, as she approached. A good deal cleaner than usual, too. Her long dark hair was recently brushed—even, maybe, washed—and she wore what Verity had once described as her best skirt, of patterned corduroy with vivid orange, yellow and turquoise flowers, and beneath what was undoubtedly a Liberty's shawl of peacock feathers, she wore what looked like a new and pristine brown polo-neck.

The reason became apparent as soon as Kirsty reached the door of the caravan, as a handsome dark-bearded man in tattered jeans and a black sweater came out, carrying a brimming cardboard box, saying, 'This lot can go, Perd. You don't need any of it. I'm dumping it *now*.'

Decisive as well as handsome, Kirsty saw. She was thankful. Perdita could do with an effective man in her life.

How wrong she was to feel pleased, she discovered in the next few seconds.

Perdita spotted her. She looked horrified. Guilty, too. And unmistakably scared.

'Oh, Miss Holt,' she said flatly. 'I wasn't expecting

you. H—hello. Um. Er—Tim, this is Miss Holt from the hospital. My friend, Tim Barclay.' She swallowed again. 'How nice to see you,' she added unconvincingly.

Kirsty could hardly remember anyone looking less pleased to see her. It occurred to her, too, that, although it was four days since Perdita had seen her daughter, she hadn't, so far, enquired how she was, or shown any sign of anxiety that Kirsty might be bringing alarming news about Verity. She wasn't, of course, but most parents would jump to an instant conclusion that she might be, and a normal first remark would almost certainly have been, 'Is Verity all right?'

'Verity isn't doing at all badly, considering her condition when she was admitted. I looked in to ask when you'd be coming in to visit her again—she misses you, you know.'

Perdita looked if possible even more guilty and uneasy.

Tim Barclay spoke for her. 'Perdita won't be coming in for a week or two,' he said firmly and with absolute assurance.

Kirsty didn't any longer care for his decisiveness at all.

'She's coming away with me for a holiday for a couple of weeks,' he went on. 'Now Verity's safely in the hospital having her treatment, Perd can get away and get a bit of a break herself. We're off as soon as the traffic clears.'

Briefly, Kirsty contemplated going into battle on Verity's behalf, but with the two of them against her there was no chance of winning, and she might alienate Perdita finally. She had no powers to stop

Perdita leaving, there was nothing she or anyone could do if Perdita chose to go away for a fortnight—or for ever? Was Verity going to see her mother again?

Tim spoke again on Perdita's behalf. 'Perd's written to Verity to explain,' he said. 'Haven't you, love?'

'That's right. And I got a stamp and posted it, too.' Clearly this represented something of an achievement.

'I suppose you couldn't drop in at the hospital on your way, to say goodbye?' Kirsty enquired, though without much hope.

'We'll see how we go,' Tim told her.

Kirsty reckoned that that meant precisely nothing, and as she drove back down Cliffside Drive to the Highcliffe entrance, her heart bled for Verity. It had always been on the cards—they had discussed it more than once—that Perdita would abandon her daughter, and that when Verity's treatment was completed and she was ready for discharge, she'd have to be taken into care. Kirsty had hated the idea when it had first been mentioned, and she hated it now, as it came unmistakably nearer. At the same time, she blamed herself. If she'd acted differently, been more assertive, perhaps she would have been able to stop Perdita leaving. She knew this was nonsense, but the knowledge didn't prevent her from feeling both guilty and depressed.

If Grant had been there, instead of herself, he would have done something. The force of his personality would have stopped Perdita in her tracks, and she'd have come obediently to the hospital to see Verity that evening.

Don't be daft, woman, Kirsty told herself, driving down the drive to the Old Stables. Perdita might have promised him anything, but she'd still have left with Tim. She'd tell Grant about what had happened in the morning, first thing, she decided, and with this tiny crumb of comfort she parked the Escort and let herself into the Old Stables.

CHAPTER EIGHT

FRAN, looking fetching in her flowery leggings with a tangerine silk shirt, her hair fluffy from washing, was not only in, but actually in the kitchen getting ahead with the evening meal.

'Time I cooked for *you*,' she remarked astoundingly. 'I saw you had mince in the freezer, so I thought I'd do pasta and salad—all right?'

'Oh, yes. You're an angel.'

'No, I'm not. I ought to have done it more often while I've been here. You're working all day. I should be cherishing you with good food, instead of swanning around having myself a great time. Good-time girl, that's me. But I'm turning over a new leaf.'

Kirsty had heard this before. At least once in any holiday, Fran was overcome by conscience and turned over a new leaf. In future, she would announce, she was to be a reformed character. What was different about today was that the words were accompanied by action.

'I can do a great pasta,' she assured Kirsty. 'It's one of my specials—you'll see. No, I don't need any help at all. Go away. Have a shower and change or something, and then come down and put your feet up.'

Bemused, Kirsty did as she was told.

Fran's bolognese sauce was as good as she'd promised—she'd been lavish with mushrooms and tomato, she'd done a mound of perfectly cooked spaghetti, and made a superb salad.

What there didn't seem to be was grated cheese, and Kirsty was deliberating whether to mention this when Fran discovered its absence for herself.

'My God, I've gone and forgotten the cheese again.' She leapt to her feet. 'Sorry. Coming up.' She crossed into the kitchen, rummaged in the refrigerator, and then turned round and began searching. 'Where on earth's your grater?'

'In the drawer next to the sink. Shall I——?'

'You just stay put. I'm doing OK.'

After a short period of mutterings, clattering and explosions of swearing, she returned and deposited a bowl of grated cheese on the table. 'Help yourself. Sorry about the hold-up.'

'This is truly yummy. Thanks a lot—just what I needed.'

'You look worn out, you know. Don't you ever stop working? You're exactly like Dad, you realise that? You should make some time just for yourself now and again, you really should.'

Fran was genuinely concerned, even worried, Kirsty saw. 'It's not usually as bad as this,' she pointed out. 'You've just happened to be here at the launch of the new service, that's all. Once we've got it going, it won't be nearly so hectic.'

Fran shook her head. 'You sound like Dad again. He always has a cast-iron reason for being rushed off his feet, and it's always going to be temporary and short-lived, though it never is. First Dad, now you. If you ask me, anyone who works in medicine needs their head examined.'

Kirsty smiled at her across the table. 'I love my job, you know. That's what makes the difference.

And so does Dad. That's a huge bonus in anyone's life.'

Fran scowled. 'I suppose. If you say so. That's what Toby said, too. Look, Kirsty, there's something I must talk to you about.'

'Go ahead, love.'

'It's not that easy. You see——' She paused, heaved a great sigh, and filled her mouth with a forkful of pasta, frowning.

Kirsty recognised the signs. Fran had fallen for someone unsuitable, and she was going to talk about him, in exuberant detail, for the rest of the evening.

She finally swallowed her mouthful, and began again. 'I always said I'd never get permanently involved with a doctor or a surgeon,' she announced.

So it was someone from St Mark's. That was a relief, and Kirsty was truly thankful. He was not going to turn out to be a drug addict she'd picked up at one of Halchester's sleazier discos. Instead it would be someone she'd met at the Lamb when Toby had taken her there. And as for permanently, Kirsty would believe that when it happened. Fran's love-life was littered with past heart-throbs who'd been permanent and for ever for several months, only to be succeeded by a newer and wildly more exciting candidate.

'So who've you met from St Mark's?' she enquired cheerfully. 'Someone I know, I expect. Tell all.'

The question seemed to throw Fran, who gulped, fidgeted with her salad, and began picking at the tablecloth. 'Well,' she said, and paused. 'You must know everyone there, I suppose.'

'Hardly. It's a big hospital. I suppose I must know

most of the medical staff, at least by sight, and nearly all the surgical consultants, but not all of them. And certainly not all the new housemen, for instance. So who is it, love?' She smiled encouragingly. It was unlike Fran to be so hesitant about disclosing every detail of the man of the moment—normally she rushed to press Kirsty to join her in admiring every characteristic of the latest paragon. Could it possibly be someone much older? In that case, she might be expecting Kirsty to disapprove. It couldn't be Grant, could it? The possibility shot into her head, refused to be dislodged, and it was Kirsty's turn to flinch as an icy hand clutched her.

The sudden silence was interrupted by the telephone at which Fran immediately leapt, almost as though to a saviour, Kirsty thought. She was chilled with a desperate foreboding, but surely she had to be wrong. Fran couldn't be going around with Grant.

Whoever was on the telephone was obviously one of Fran's London friends, and female at that, wanting to know why she wasn't there for the start of some course.

'It won't really matter if I miss the first day or two,' Fran was protesting.

The voice on the other end clearly thought it would.

'Well, I can't be there. No way.' Fran scowled at the telephone. 'You'll simply have to make my excuses, say I'm out of London until next week.'

The caller didn't like this, and said so.

'Well, I'm sorry, truly I am, that it does mean you'll be on your own for the start, but you'll be all right, for Pete's sake. No one'll eat you.'

Kirsty, seeing that the conversation was likely to be prolonged, began to clear the table and fill the dishwasher. The counter-tops, as ever if Fran cooked, looked as if a ten-course banquet for twenty at least had been prepared—she seemed to have used every pan, bowl, chopping-board and implement, and Kirsty was still making a clearance when Fran at last came off the telephone and erupted into the kitchen, conscience-stricken.

'You weren't meant to do any of that. I was going to see to it all this evening. You were meant to sit around polishing your nails or watching the box.'

'I had a super meal, it was really great, and I'm not going to collapse from exhaustion filling the dishwasher. Coffee?'

'No, I can't wait. I'll have to rush—I'm running late now.'

'Before you go, what's all this about being in London for a course?'

'Oh, it's nothing, it doesn't matter one bit. Joanne's just fussing because she'll be on her own for the first few days, but she doesn't need me to hold her hand, blow that.'

'But what course is it, and where? You never said——'

'It's silly. It's only a cookery course Dad made me put my name down for. He said if I wasn't going to do some sort of training, I must either get a job, or do a proper cookery course. He wouldn't let me have the fare to California for Christmas unless I did, he said. So I persuaded Joanne—you remember her, she was at school—to do this ten-week cordon bleu thing. But it's not going to matter in the least if I miss the first few days. Joanne can bring me up to date on it.'

'But what's Dad going to say?'

'Oh, I'll talk him round. He won't mind me missing the odd day as long as I do the course. He'll hardly notice, I don't suppose, as long as no one reminds him. And I'm not going back to London this week, that's definite. Don't *you* start nagging, there's a love. Everything's under control, I'm not going to cut the course, I'll be there in London next week, I promise. Gosh, I must fly, I'm fearfully late—the meal took longer than I thought it would. See you tomorrow.' She snatched up her mohair scarf and the bulging satchel that travelled everywhere with her, and fled.

Kirsty took a deep breath. Fran was clearly up to something—but then, she always was. She had a crush, or was having an affair. Since her sister had been about fourteen, Kirsty had seldom been able to decide which of these descriptions applied to Fran's feverish relationships with the opposite sex. But there was nothing new or in the least surprising about this, and it wasn't likely to be Fran who got hurt, if anyone did. Fran would be up and down, miserable one day, over the moon the next, but then, inevitably, she'd fall as suddenly out of love as she'd fallen in, and there'd be a brief period of calm before the cycle began again. As of now she'd obviously gone right overboard for someone—for one of the doctors at St Mark's—that, she had managed to spell out.

But not, surely not, for Grant. Surely he couldn't, wouldn't, it wasn't possible that——

'No,' Kirsty said aloud. 'No. I don't believe this. I'm making it up. There's not the remotest reason to suppose Fran is in any way involved with Grant, of all people. Stop it.'

Over in St Mark's, Grant was in fact sitting quietly in the canteen with Quentin, having a quick cup of coffee with a belated sandwich. They had missed supper, and were snatching a fast snack before returning to the ward, where they had a difficult admission.

On the far side of the huge area, Toby sat alone, drinking coffee and drumming his fingers on the table. He looked worried and edgy, and Quentin, who was feeling much more comfortable and relaxed with Grant recently, made a comment he wouldn't have risked a week earlier.

'He looks jumpy, Toby Gresham, doesn't he? Over there, by the swing doors.'

Grant's eyes swivelled. He hadn't noticed Toby was anywhere in the place, but sure enough, there he was, on the other side of the canteen. And as Grant watched, Toby rose, his face lit up and he looked entirely different, as a vision in tangerine silk and flowery leggings, topped by an aureole of golden curls, surged in and flew ecstatically into his welcoming arms.

Fran. Grant and Quentin were both riveted, as the two clutched and kissed, and finally sat down together at the table. As they watched, though, the joy and ecstasy evaporated before their eyes. Toby's concentrated expression as he put a searching question on a ward round was familiar, and both his watchers could see he'd switched from delight to interrogation. A relentless interrogation. Of an uneasy, apologetic Fran.

She shook her head, spread her hands dramatically, looked at him large-eyed and apparently woebegone.

To their considerable surprise, Toby unmistakably began to tick her off. He thumped the table, scowled at her, and spoke vehemently and fast.

'The course of true love hardly seems to be running smoothly tonight,' Quentin remarked sarcastically. He was not sorry to see Toby, who made so many daily problems for him, having a few troubles of his own. Quentin hadn't found Toby easy to work for, or particularly likeable.

'True love?' Grant was seized by a sudden overwhelming anxiety. 'Do you mean those two are having some sort of affair?'

'I'll say. Haven't you heard?' Quentin could hardly believe Grant knew nothing about it. 'It's been the talk of the hospital—they're everywhere together. In and out wherever you turn. Here, the Lamb, that block of flats at the foot of Cliffside Drive where Toby lives. Everyone's seen them—she's more or less living at Toby's flat, they say, though of course in theory she's staying with her sister. And God knows what *she* can be making of it all. How they both can do it to her, no one can understand. However, they seem to be having a few differences this evening, wouldn't you say?'

'Agreed.' Grant snapped the word out, and then his lips compressed into a thin line.

He'd gone too far, Quentin realised at once. He shouldn't have attempted to regale Grant with the latest hot gossip. 'Oh, well,' he said uneasily, 'I suppose it'll all sort itself out. Perhaps I'd better go and check on the patient now.'

'Do that,' Grant said absently, though, as Quentin duly noticed, his eyes remained fixed on the couple by the swing doors.

So Grant was interested, whatever he might pretend, Quentin told himself as he departed.

What Quentin never for one moment suspected was that Grant hardly knew how to contain himself. He wanted, immediately, both to batter Toby to pulp and to take Kirsty into his arms and comfort her, tell her everything was going to be all right, never mind, my love, you're well rid of him and I'll look after you for ever. He also contemplated giving Fran a piece of his mind, throwing her bodily into his car, and driving her straight back to her neglectful parent in Harley Street. Yet even while all this whirled furiously around in his head, he longed to be able to turn it into a non-happening, somehow to be able to dissolve the actuality of Toby and Fran at the table across the room, and, even at the cost of his own anguish, restore Toby safely to Kirsty, remould him as her loving and devoted partner. Anything was better than this, that Toby should not only have abandoned her, but betrayed her publicly, making her a laughing-stock.

He didn't know how to bear the knowledge that the entire hospital was engaged in gossiping maliciously—and delightedly—about Toby's treatment of her. She was his beloved, his forever love, and if he had to lose her, if she chose someone else, that someone had to show he was worthy of her.

There was nothing he could do. Nothing whatever. He couldn't destroy Toby, or restore him to

Kirsty. He couldn't even put a stop to Fran's behaviour. He couldn't change anything. He was powerless—he couldn't even stop the gossip.

Wait a minute, though. There was something. He could give them something else to gossip about, couldn't he?

What if he and Kirsty were to have a blazing affair, publicly and openly in front all those curious eyes? Then Toby and Fran would drop to becoming a mere sideshow. If he handled it right, it might look as though Toby's affair with Fran was no more than his response to being dropped by Kirsty in favour of her new love. Himself. Grant suddenly shoved his chair back and strode purposefully across the canteen towards the exit, his jaw jutting menacingly, oblivious now to everyone in the vicinity.

All he had to do, he was deciding, was to behave naturally. He wouldn't be deceiving Kirsty, he'd be doing only what he'd wanted to do ever since he'd first met her. He had held back because of some stupid old-world notion of—of what? It was difficult to recollect the reasoning that had seemed so powerful at the time, that he had no right to stroll in and disrupt a relationship that had stood the test of the years.

He had forced himself to stand back, given himself a hard time, and all for nothing. The relationship had fallen apart, destroyed by that miserable Toby Gresham himself—and in a blaze of publicity that was unforgivable.

His other asinine reason for resisting his love for Kirsty had been that he saw it as an obligation, as the newly appointed consultant, not to sweep in and steal, not only the hoped-for post, but also his girl from that unspeakable Toby. His mouth twisted. A fine waste of time and effort that had been. And it had cost him, too. He remembered the pain he'd endured each time he'd turned dutifully away from Kirsty. His own beloved. She'd been his from the beginning, his own true love, and he'd seen it from their first encounter, and yet had stupidly tried to turn his back on what the gods offered.

He and Kirsty belonged together. Now the way ahead was clear.

He was going straight off to claim her. They'd make wild tumultuous love at last, and they'd share their innermost thoughts, too. It would go on, the loving and the sharing, to the end of his days.

The car keys in his hand, he stood in the darkness with the lighted hospital behind him, and took an uneasy step back.

Of course it wasn't too late to call on her. It couldn't be much more than eight or nine in the evening, a perfectly reasonable hour to go and see anyone—though perhaps he should ring first. He glanced at his watch. To his astonishment, it was already past nine-thirty. Well, definitely he should ring first, not just turn up on the doorstep.

What was he going to say?

Come out for a drink, the night is young? Or, perhaps, can I come and see you, there's something I have to tell you?

Like what? Like, I love you forever, or like, that two-timing Toby is having it off with your sister, and I can't bear it?

What was he going to tell Kirsty about Toby and Fran, in any case? He sighed heavily. It was more complicated than he had thought at first. He owed

Kirsty total honesty, even at the cost of hurting her.

He could ring her and tell her the truth. I need to talk to you, he would say, can I come round? And then he'd take it from there.

But he had this child in the ward, and Quentin expecting him. Anxiously and nervily, no doubt, watching the clock and wondering what was keeping him. He couldn't leave Quentin to cope for the rest of the night by himself, he'd have a nervous breakdown, and as for the child. . .

No way. He didn't know how he could have forgotten the new admission, even for five minutes.

Sombrely, he put the car keys back in his pocket, turned on his heel, and retraced his steps.

CHAPTER NINE

KIRSTY went miserably to bed, and rose in the morning as desolate and uncertain as she'd been the previous evening. Impatient with herself for permitting this fictional anxiety to dominate her, she made herself strong black coffee and ate her muesli while having another go at ringing her father to try to find out how much it mattered whether Fran attended her class from its opening. But, just the same as the night before, all she could get was his answerphone offering instructions about which hospital to ring for his registrar or secretary.

She had half an hour to fill in before her first call—the mother had asked her not to arrive until she'd packed the other children off to school—so, as she had time in hand, she decided to look in on Mrs Anstruther. She hadn't seen her for several days, and the old lady was always up and eating her breakfast well before eight—and enjoyed an early visitor, too.

Mrs Anstruther was delighted to see her, offered her toast and marmalade, which Kirsty declined, and instead offered her a bowl of apples from the garden.

'Russets, only picked yesterday, you'll like them. It's still too early to pick the Cox's—when we do, you shall have a basket of them.'

Kirsty thanked her, and asked if she could do any shopping for her. 'I'm doing some for myself anyway, so it wouldn't be the least trouble.'

Mrs Anstruther assured her that both fridge and freezer were bursting with supplies of everything she could possibly need. 'Too much, really. I always overstock, as if I were still feeding a family. You mustn't hesitate to ask, if you ever run short.'

'I'll remember. And thank you for the apples, we'll both enjoy them. I hope Fran isn't being a nuisance, or making a lot of noise late at night? She can sometimes be a bit thoughtless.'

'My dear, she's no trouble whatever. I hardly know she's here. She must be creeping about. I never hear her come in at night, and in the morning I don't hear a thing until she comes back here after her breakfast in your place, when she has her shower and goes out.'

'Oh, good, I'm glad to hear it. It's super of you to have taken her in—now I must be off myself. See you.' She spoke cheerfully, but took the apples back to the Old Stables with her mind whirling. Mrs Anstruther's description of Fran's comings and goings, so unobtrusive and silent, and her arrival after breakfast, had cast a sudden blinding light over what her sister must be up to. She'd been slow, Kirsty realised, hopelessly and pathetically slow, not to mention gullible, not to have spotted it sooner. She ought to know Fran well enough to have guessed that she wasn't sleeping at Highcliffe at all: she was staying with this unknown doctor in his flat in Halchester. That explained why she'd been so eager to arrange a separate bedroom for herself, away from the Old Stables, so that Kirsty couldn't any longer monitor her comings and goings.

She'd gone out of her way, too, Kirsty

remembered, to stress that she'd be able to have a good lie-in over at the big house, and then, after Kirsty had left, she'd come across and get her own breakfast lateish—she was on holiday, after all, and she'd enjoy long, lazy mornings.

Just as Fran had intended, Kirsty had been completely taken in. Absent-mindedly, she dumped the russets on the counter-top in her kitchen. She was worried. She hadn't been exactly alarmed or concerned to hear Fran was madly in love with some unknown doctor—unless, of course, it happened to be Grant, and surely she must be wrong about that? Fran was always falling in and out of love, but if she had moved in with this unknown, it mattered who he was, what sort of reputation he had. What was more, at least she began to doubt that the man in question could really be Grant. That surely must have been no more than yesterday's mad nightmare, as she'd kept telling herself at the time. For surely Grant wouldn't be living with Fran in the publicity of Long Barn? If he had been, the whole hospital would have known. No, it must be one of the senior housemen or a registrar.

But who was it? Kirsty felt elder sisterly, responsible—and neglectful. She told herself this was silly. After all, Fran was over twenty, and she'd been on the Pill for years.

She'd have to check up, put herself out and discover exactly who it was that Fran was going around with. She'd find out at lunchtime, that would be it. She'd go across to the Lamb for a sandwich, and ask around. People would be bound to know.

That decision taken, she put Fran on hold in the

back of her mind, and set out on her morning calls. They took longer than she'd planned, as they nearly always did. With the home-care service still in its early days, she had come to the conclusion that it was worth spending plenty of time on these first assessment visits—which most of this morning's were—but they did tend to over-run and use up a vast amount of her day. This morning she also had to fit in a call on one of the family doctors, at the end of his morning surgery. He had been uneasy about a little girl who had been moved back into her parents' flat, and who was a patient of his, saying she wasn't suitable for home care and neither were her parents—he was obviously, they'd agreed after the case conference, terrified that looking after her was going to disrupt both his day's work and his night's sleep with constant alarm calls. It also meant his district nurse, who already had too much on her plate, would be heavily overloaded.

Kirsty couldn't help wondering whether the district nurse would relish being labelled as 'his district nurse'. All right, she was allocated to his practice, but she would undoubtedly consider herself a professional in her own right, rather than the property of the practice. However, as she went in to see him, she decided to play it his way on this, their first meeting, and she embarked on an exposition of the daily timetable they'd worked out for the patient, with visits from the district nurse and nurses from the home-care service dovetailing.

This worked, and Dr Fortescue back-pedalled. 'It does begin to look as if you're going to be providing a fair amount of support from St Mark's,' he admitted. 'I was afraid it was all going to be down to us. Perhaps you could go into these schedules with Jane Morris herself, and see what she feels.'

As Jane Morris was the lady previously referred to as 'my district nurse', Kirsty chalked up a point to female solidarity.

At the end of her visit, Dr Fortescue escorted her to the front door himself, thanked her for sparing an hour from her busy day, told her how much he appreciated her trouble in giving him such an illuminating account of the aims and methods of the new service. He was sure they'd be able to work together as a team, he'd keep in touch, and he looked forward to meeting her again. He shook hands with warm friendliness. 'Goodbye—take care,' he cried, standing on the doorstep and waving as she turned out of the drive.

That had ben well worth while, but here she was, still with two more visits to fit in before lunch. When they had been completed she was truly behind schedule, and realised she was hardly going to be able to spend the long, gossipy lunch-hour in the Lamb she'd been planning, chatting up all and sundry and finding out who was going around with Fran.

She drove into St Mark's car park, and decided to make straight for lunch, and go to the office afterwards. She had locked the Escort, and was turning to walk over to the Lamb, when she heard someone call her name. Uncertainly, she hesitated, and looked about her, and then saw Toby, at the hospital entrance, waving energetically.

She waved cheerfully back. Probably he was on his way to the Lamb, too. They could lunch together, and she could tell him about Fran—maybe he would know who it was who was involved with her.

He came towards her at a brisk trot. 'I've been trying to get hold of you all morning,' he said. 'Come and have lunch, we need to have a talk.' He took her by the arm, and urged her towards his own car. 'We'll go in my car.'

'Can't we just eat in the Lamb? That's where I was going.'

'No, come to the flat with me. I bought sandwiches earlier, and I'll make coffee. All right? The Lamb's no good, all those ears flapping and eyes on stalks. Come on, love, this is quite important.'

Whatever could it be? More problems, as if she hadn't enough already. 'I can't be too long,' she warned him. 'I haven't been into the office yet, and then I've loads of afternoon calls.'

'It needn't take long,' he said firmly, unlocking the BMW and opening the passenger door for her. 'Hop in, there's a good girl.'

Toby's flat was as familiar to her as the Old Stables—in fact, she herself had been largely responsible for its colour schemes and much of its more mundane equipment, Toby concentrating on the larger and more interesting items. It was in a modern block at the foot of Cliffside Drive, with wide jutting balconies and huge picture windows overlooking the sea—freezing cold in winter.

He led the way inside and across to the lift. 'I got sandwiches you like,' he told her, as they entered it. 'Salmon and watercress, and then Brie in walnut bread with tomato and cuccumber, and I bought some grapes, too. I'll put the coffee straight on, and then we can settle down and talk.' He unlocked the front door, and made for the kitchen. 'Make yourself comfortable,' he said. 'I won't be a minute.'

Whatever could it be that he wanted to talk about so privately? Horrors, he hadn't gone back to his earlier ideas about buying a house, had he? That might account for why he didn't want to talk about it in the Lamb, where, it was true, the very walls had ears. Had he seen somewhere he'd fallen for?

He came in with a plate of sandwiches and a dish of grapes. 'Coffee up in a sec,' he said, and retired again behind the open shelving that separated his kitchen from the wide living-room.

Kirsty sank down on the squashy leather sofa that he had bought to celebrate his appointment as senior registrar, stretched out her legs comfortably, and gazed through the floor-to-ceiling sliding doors across to the Channel, sparkling in the midday sun. 'This is great,' she said lazily. 'Lovely and peaceful, too—much nicer here than at the Lamb, I do agree.'

He came back with his glass coffee-pot, and poured into the glass mugs that went with it. 'Black, as usual?'

'Please.'

He sat down opposite her on the Charles Eames leather chair that he'd purchased second-hand from a departing registrar, whose new wife hadn't cared for it, and surveyed her. 'Look,' he said, 'this isn't going to be easy, I'm afraid.'

He'd succeeded in startling her. 'Why on earth not?' It was unlike him to be nervous and on edge with her, so she could see now that in fact he was. 'Is something wrong?'

'No, no. On the contrary. It's just that I ought to have told you before. The thing is—well, I—we—that is, Fran was supposed to tell you, only she kept putting it off, so in the end I decided it was up to me.' He paused, still on edge, Kirsty could see.

What was all this about? At least he seemed to know what Fran was up to, that was something—only why was he worried about it? That wasn't too hopeful.

'At least you seem to know what Fran's doing, that's what I've been wanting to know. Who is it she's going around with? Is it someone—oh, I know it sounds dreadfully quaint and old-world, and silly—but is it someone suitable? She thinks she's so sophisticated, but sometimes she hasn't a clue, and——'

'I don't know whether you'll think it's suitable or not, that's the problem. That's why I got you here. Thing is, it's me.' He eyed her exactly like a small boy caught at the fridge with the Black Forest gâteau.

'*You*?' The information certainly rocked her. 'You, Toby?' she repeated, staring at him wide-eyed with astonishment.

He looked back at her, suddenly very still and tense. 'Yes,' he said. 'Me. I've gone and fallen in love with your sister Fran.'

'You mean it's been you she's been rushing off to meet?'

'Yes. I don't know why she didn't tell you from the beginning—in fact, I didn't realise she hadn't, to begin with, and then she kept saying she would, but somehow she never did.'

'Typical Fran,' Kirsty commented unthinkingly,

and smiled radiantly. 'Oh, Toby, what a huge relief, you've no idea. I've been worried half out of my mind in case she'd taken up with someone frightful, and all the while it's been you.' Theatrically, she fanned herself, laughed happily, and added, 'So that's all right, then.'

For a brief moment, Toby had eyed her uncertainly, but then she saw him relax as much as she had. He took an enormous bite of his sandwich, which until then he hadn't touched, and through a full mouth said something she couldn't catch.

'Sorry?'

He swallowed. 'I said, attagirl. Kirsty, love, you're the greatest. I should have trusted you to understand—after all, you always have.'

His eyes were no longer wary; instead, they shone with a clear light she'd never noticed before.

Correction. She had seen it before. Once. When he'd finally decided he could afford the BMW.

Oh, help. What a ghastly thought to have about him. It might be a useful one, though, Because if—when—Fran fell out of love with him, as she almost inevitably would in a few months, perhaps he wouldn't be too badly hurt. She hoped. Anyway, she couldn't warn him that with Fran it might not last, that usually it didn't. It would be unkind, and maybe she was wrong. Perhaps this would be the real thing at last for them both. Fran might be growing up. Toby might turn out to be the love of her life. What's more, he might even be able to cope with her. It wasn't beyond the bounds of possibility. She smiled at him again with genuine joy, and exclaimed, 'Oh, Toby, isn't this great? Truly great.

I can't think of anyone I'd sooner have for a brother-in-law.'

He gave her a look straight from his heart. 'Me, too. I mean, for brother read sister. And it is honestly all right? You don't—um—you don't feel I've let you down?'

'Let me down? Of course not. After all, whatever the hospital grapevine likes to imagine, we've never been in love, have we? You're the greatest friend I've ever had, but the strength of it, I'd say, has been partly because we weren't in love.' At one point, certainly, she had been afraid he'd been on the edge of falling for her, but it hadn't happened after all, and now it never would. Thank the lord for Fran, appearing just when she was needed—and maybe this time it would last.

'I don't suppose she mentioned it,' she began, realising that she had someone now to share the problem of Fran, someone, indeed, who might actually be able to influence her far more effectively than her older sister ever could, 'but she should have been back in London for the beginning of a cookery course this week?'

'This week?' He stared. 'No, not a word. She's the scattiest creature, isn't she? I must be mad, but I have to admit I find it endearing. She did say she ought to be back in Harley Street this weekend, so I said I'd change my weekend off, and drive her up.'

'Oh, good.' If he said he would, he undoubtedly would. And it probably didn't matter if Fran missed a couple of days.

'Oh, Kirsty, I've never felt like this before.' It was an explosion, and his eyes blazed across the room at her. 'I—I adore her, you know. I can see in so many ways she's the silliest thing around, but that makes me love her all the more. I want to see she's all right forever, would you believe? It doesn't sound much like me, does it? I used to be the one who looked out for me and my future career. But I can't think about anything, now, except Fran, and if she's going to be all right.'

'That's lovely. I'm so very pleased for you both.' Kirsty stood up, walked round the coffee-table and hugged him. 'I can't tell you how wonderful it's going to be to know you're going to be looking out for her—instead of me trying from a distance and failing hopelessly.' She glanced at her watch. 'And now I dare say we'd better take ourselves back to the treadmill rather fast, and think about an afternoon's work.'

'I suppose so,' he agreed dreamily. He looked at his own watch. 'Good grief, I'll say we'd better. Come on.'

Flushed and happy, Kirsty erupted into the office, to find Grant there before her.

'Oh, am I late?' she exclaimed. 'Have I kept you waiting? I'm dreadfully sorry.'

'Not at all. I've hardly been here more than a minute or two, and in any case, Dinah has been putting me in the picture most adequately over the Nicholson family, whom I gather you saw yesterday.' His tone was formal, his eyes guarded. Inwardly he was bleeding. He'd been in the car park and watched her depart in Toby's BMW, presumably for lunch. He'd decided that Toby, who had looked a little anxious, might very likely be going to break the news at last to her about his affair with her sister.

He'd expected Kirsty to turn up in the office upset, subdued, trying to hide her anguish.

But no way. Bright-eyed and bushy-tailed, she was inescapably in the highest of spirits, and Grant saw at once what must have happened. That two-timing Toby had simply given her a good lunch and chatted her up, to put her on hold, and Kirsty had swallowed it. She was happy, no doubt about it, and Grant hadn't the slightest idea what he could do. How could he break in, tell her the truth about her sister and Toby Gresham, and destroy her confidence completely?

On the other hand, how could he not? She had to know. He couldn't stand by, watch this, and let it go on, while half St Mark's sniggered.

She was talking about the Nicholsons. 'An amazing house, Dinah, you were right about that. They've changed the inside of it completely for Zoe's return home. They're two devoted, worrying parents, falling over backwards to do the right thing by her, panicking away non-stop in case they're failing her, guilty because they've let her have her way and live at home, worried out of their minds all the time, and if you ask me, it's their worry that's giving her asthma. Zoe says that herself, and she's not helped at all by Dr Hardcastle, another worry-guts.'

'How about her school attendance?' Grant asked. 'Is that adding to the problems, do you suppose?'

'She's a rather academic child, I suspect. Anyway, she says the teaching is brilliant compared with Northcliffe's, and the standard much higher. She seems to be enjoying that no end, to be stimulated rather than stressed. What is upsetting her is the atmosphere of fuss at home, and there she does compare Northcliffe to advantage—she says that there, having asthma was normal, taken for granted, the kids were expected to cope with it, and this was in fact a help, though she didn't cotton on to it until she came home, where even so much as the suspicion of a wheeze provokes crisis action. Then she starts to panic herself, and she can feel it all going out of control, yet not be able to stop it.'

Grant nodded. 'I reckon that's what must have happened when we had her in Cas, and I admitted her.'

'Well, first she'd had her parents getting hysterical, insisting on ringing up Dr Hardcastle, and then, when he arrived, he was the opposite of calming or reassuring. Instead he went into crisis mode himself, insisting on ringing for an ambulance and getting her to hospital fast—that's when she feels she totally lost control of her breathing.'

Grant pulled a face. 'Oh, dear, here I am, encouraging the family doctors not to hesitate to ask for admission if they think an asthmatic might need it—don't keep them at home too long, I urge them. And now look what happens—we can't win, can we?'

'You won all right with Zoe,' Kirsty assured him. 'She has complete confidence in you. You helped her to relax and get her breathing back under control. That evening in the ward, you sat by her, and that was when she knew it was going to be all right.' She'd wanted to tell him this, but she had to come clean about the next bit as well, and that might not please him at all. 'I told her that another time, she should get her parents to ring us, and one of us would come at any time. I said you'd come yourself if she needed you—I thought that would be the ultimate reassurance, and it was.'

He wasn't annoyed. 'Of course I'll go and see her. If we can break the cycle of parents and Dr Hardcastle panicking, and keep Zoe in her own home and her asthma under control, we'll have solved her problem. Her parents—and even Bob Hardcastle—may calm down and get used to having her at home with a bit of asthma, and we won't need to think about other arrangements for her. I'll go at any time, and you can tell her parents so.'

'Oh, if you just appeared a couple of times as soon as they so much as began to worry, that would probably do the trick. Mrs Nicholson adores Zoe, and she loves having her at home. She's just scared she's harming her by having her there.'

'Perhaps if you go and see Zoe, we should send Kirsty to placate Dr Hardcastle,' Dinah suggested. 'She has a magic touch with irate GPs, it seems to me,' She grinned.

It didn't go down well. Grant scowled ferociously. 'I think you may safely leave me to deal with Dr Hardcastle,' he snapped. The picture of Kirsty going round the district soothing general practitioners upset him, he had no idea why. But it wasn't on. Hastily he switched subject. 'What's the latest on the Weybournes?'

'I'm seeing Kevin this evening,' Kirsty said.

'What time?'

'I'm told he usually arrives soon after six-thirty, on his way home, so I've said I'll be there on the ward then.'

'Good. I'll still be here then, so I can see him with you, and we'll try to get to the root of whatever it is that's bugging the family, shall we?'

Kirsty's heart lifted, though she replied soberly that Grant's presence would be very helpful, she was sure.

'Then afterwards we can have a meal and see what we think about what he's said, how would that be?' He sounded as confident as he had every right to be, but he looked across the desk uneasily, praying that Kirsty wouldn't immediately inform him that she was booked for dinner with Toby.

In fact, although she was over the moon, she merely nodded, and remarked coolly that that would be very nice.

'See you, then.' Grant decided not to tempt fate further. He looked at his watch. 'Quentin will be wondering where I've got to,' he added, and took himself off.

'Well, aren't you the lucky one?' Dinah commented enviously. 'I sure hope he'll take you somewhere super, not just plonk you down in the canteen, that's all.'

'I'll tell you in the morning,' Kirsty said lightly, not admitting that she couldn't have cared less where they were to eat. Even the canteen would be sheer heaven.

They'd be together, they were talking again, the world was wonderful.

At the end of her afternoon calls, hardly admitting to herself that there was anything unusual in what she was doing, she fitted in a stop at the Old Stables, where she showered and changed.

Mustn't overdo it. She could hardly turn up in the ward to talk to Kevin Weybourne looking overdue for Ascot or opera at Glyndebourne—and what if they ended up in the canteen, munching sandwiches? But she yearned to be some sort of knock-out—if only she had Fran's gift for dress, she'd possess the right gear to wow them and yet remain coolly casual. Fran was so good on fashion—a pity, Kirsty thought, that she'd not had the time to take advantage of this during her stay. They could have shopped in Halchester's boutiques, and, with Fran's eye, picked out a couple of outfits to carry Kirsty anywhere from the canteen to Le Manoir du Quat' Saisons.

However, it had not been merely lack of time or opportunity that had prevented them shopping together, she thought affectionately. Fran had had her eye elsewhere than on fashionable outfits for her sister. On Toby. Perhaps that love might even last. Kirsty did pray it would—it would be great to have Fran settled and Toby actually in the family—but even as she speculated so hopefully, it struck her as wildly improbable that those two would still be together five years from now, let alone fifty.

Still riffling through her wardrobe, she reached a decision, and stepped into a skirt that had done duty for day or evening, summer or winter, for the last few years. It was still the right length, though, had a sophisticated design of black on white, and it would go anywhere. Always had. She wore a black blouse with it for sobriety, but in see-through chiffon for the triumph of hope over expectation, and a serious black waistcoat as an insurance policy. Then she made up her face with obsessional detail, and contemplated her hair. She could hardly leave it hanging loose round her shoulders to interview Kevin in the office, that wouldn't be at all the thing.

In the end she compromised by plaiting it, but leaving the plait hanging down her back instead of fastening it on the top of her head. Assessing herself cautiously in the long mirror, she decided she'd do.

CHAPTER TEN

GRANT'S main problem had been to make up his mind whether to take Kirsty somewhere where half St Mark's could watch them eating together, or whether to take her as far away from Halchester as possible, so that he could tell her the truth about Toby and that self-centred sister of hers in utter privacy. The news was going to destroy her. She loved them both.

She'd be tired out, too, he thought angrily. A long hard day, and a hard week behind her as well. Perhaps there was no urgent necessity for her to face such pain tonight. He'd take her to Long Barn. It was Friday evening, after all, and half St Mark's would be there celebrating the approach of the weekend.

If he was seen there, making a dead set at Kirsty—no problem over that—they'd speculate even more about what was going on. But might they not begin to wonder, start asking themselves who it was who was actually making a fool of whom? Had Toby, for instance, taken up with Fran only because he'd already lost Kirsty?

A delightful, morale-boosting thought, even if he knew it wasn't true. But that was the way he'd play it, and please God it would be true one day. Feeling immensely more cheerful, he rang Long Barn, booked a table for two, ordered the dish of the day for them both, which turned out to be pheasant with green apples and Cointreau, chose a wine to go with it. Dinner with Kirsty. They could have a long leisurely meal together, Long Barn's best, and they'd talk for hours. About everything—themselves, each other, the future. The future? He must be mad.

The hours dragged. He felt like a schoolboy on the verge of his first date. At last—or so it seemed—at six-thirty, he was able to enter Kirsty's office, where she was sitting sedately behind her desk, looking wonderful, some sort of black jacket with floppy sleeves buttoned up to her neck, her hair shining.

Kevin Weybourne was sitting opposite, leaning forward and talking vehemently.

Grant drew a chair up and joined in. The conversation really took off. Kevin unburdened himself at length, and in the end, the discussion with him proved much more positive and useful than any of them had expected. They sent him on his way nearly an hour later with most of the loose ends tied, and the way ahead mapped.

'That seems reasonably hopeful,' Grant remarked. 'I suggest we mull it over while we're eating, how'd that be? Let's get out of this place fast, in any case, before either of us gets grabbed for anything else.'

'I'm all in favour,' Kirsty agreed. She rose to her feet, retrieved her bag from the filing cabinet, and walked through the door he was holding for her. She was so happy she could have exploded. They were together, with the evening stretching brilliantly ahead.

'We'll take my car, shall we?' he asked, as they

went along the corridor towards the lifts.

'Sure,' she said easily. Not the canteen, then. Better and better. She smiled radiantly into his eyes.

He followed her into the lift, his pulse racing. It raced even faster as he stood behind the thick golden plait that hung down her back, and he longed urgently to put his fingers on it, pull it apart and handle her shining blonde hair. And then, of course, handle her, and hold her to him forever.

Hastily he clamped down his over-active imagination, walking apparently placidly alongside her to his car, remarking only, 'Long Barn be all right, I hope? I took a chance and booked a table without consulting you first, I'm afraid.'

'Long Barn is always super,' she told him, and then asked herself if she'd sounded patronising.

'Also without confirming it with you,' he told her, when they were settled in the car, and he was driving out of the hospital gates, 'I went ahead and said we'd eat pheasant—they prepare them to order, one bird between the two of us. So I hope it's all right, and you like pheasant.'

'Love it—don't often get it, though. Marvellous.' She almost added that eating anything with him would be unblemished joy, but fortunately succeeded in biting the words back before they escaped. She pressed her lips together, and stared out at the familiar road leading away from St Mark's, determined not to give the game away by bursting into song.

Long Barn was packed, but their table—she was already thinking of it as their own table—was waiting for them.

'Starters?' Grant enquired.

There was smoked trout, mushrooms *en croûte*, smoked wild venison, or fresh pineapple with *fromage frais* and watercress.

'The pineapple sounds delicious.'

'It is. I've had it several times, and it's great. Right. We'll both have the pineapple.'

The Chablis Grant had ordered was already on the table. 'Would you like some wine now, or would you prefer an aperitif?' he asked.

'I'd love some wine.' I'd love absolutely anything you're offering, would have been nearer the truth, she knew, though naturally she would have died rather than let the words pass her lips. Instead, and a little forbiddingly, as if they were both sitting together in Long Barn for the sole purpose of transacting essential departmental business, she launched briskly into a discussion of the Weybourne family and Linda's future.

Earnest and locked into concentration, her eyes kept meeting Grant's across the table. They were huge and liquid, and he could have drowned in them until the end of his days.

'He's a sensible fellow, Kevin,' was his actual response. 'He's found what seems a brilliant solution to Linda's problem, if only it works—thank the lord he persuaded her to come clean with him and tell him how she really felt.'

'You were absolutely right, too, about her being lonely at home, feeling cut off from the outside world.'

'She was moving into depression—I should have spotted it.'

'So should I. I was blinded, I'm afraid, because it seemed such a triumph, getting her home to live and out of hospital. I did have cold feet that it might be too much for Jill, month after month, or that the system of part-time volunteers and nurses might break down, but that Linda herself would feel miserable and miss the hospital ward—no, it never crossed my mind. It should have done.' Kirsty shook her head.

'There's not the slightest need to blame yourself. Now we do know, though, it's perfectly understandable. For years now, ever since her injury, she's been surrounded by hospital staff and patients twenty-four hours a day. She must have found it stimulating and, compared with it, home was flat and offered no challenges.'

'We knew she'd have problems in adapting, but I'm afraid it didn't occur to me that she'd be lonely and depressed at home.'

Their pineapple arrived. It was as delicious as it had promised to be, but neither of them had their minds on it.

'Of course,' Kirsty went on, prodding absently at her pineapple, 'we had originally planned for her to go to school every day with her sisters, and if she'd been able to do that, she might have been quite OK. I was furious at the time. I felt—well, I still do—that the school could have put themselves out a little for someone like Linda, in a wheelchair for life. I was shocked when they refused to take responsibility for her on their premises.'

'I only hope this plan of Kevin's doesn't fall down at the same point—I fully understand why he doesn't want to raise Linda's hopes until he knows for sure he's pulled it off. I must see if I can unearth people who'll be able to lobby members of the board of governors.'

Kevin was trying to make arrangements for Linda to attend Halchester's fee-paying girls' grammar school. His church had embarked on an appeal for funds for her tuition, but when Kevin and the vicar had gone to see the head to discuss Linda's needs—and her scholastic record—she'd turned out to be almost as eager as they were for her to become a pupil there. She'd offered at once to waive the fees, and was putting this to the board of governors at their next meeting—she'd assured Kevin that she had every confidence they'd agree to this. If so, the way ahead would be clear, and Linda could go daily to the grammar school from the start of the spring term in January.

'If only she can,' Kirsty breathed. 'Our problem solved, but what an opening for Linda. A new life. If she could just go on to university, what a difference it would make for her entire future.' Her eyes shone.

Grant longed to kiss her. Instead he spooned up more of his pineapple, to which he'd never been so indifferent.

'I do wish Kevin had mentioned earlier what he was up to,' she went on. 'We might have been able to help—lobby the governors, as you say. I think I really must try to be in the ward one evening a week regularly to cover parents' visiting hours. I've always been ready to see them by appointment, but I reckon I ought to be around for sure on one particular evening, so that they can pop in for a chat without any forward planning.'

'There's something in that, but you must make

sure you have time off to compensate. Either finish early one afternoon, or start late one morning.'

Kirsty grinned. 'Or take an *enormous* lunch-hour,' she suggested, her eyes sparkling. 'Like here, say.'

Grant lost all interest in the Weybourne family. His horizon was filled by Kirsty. Only Kirsty, and forever. A pity, now it came to it, that they had to plough their way through this meal. To take her up to his room and make wild, ecstatic love to her, to plan the hours, and the days, and the weeks, the months and, finally, the years ahead of them—this was all he wanted to do.

Kirsty put the last of the pineapple into her enchanting mouth that he was still longing to lean across the table and kiss, and remarked, 'That was delicious. I enjoyed every single mouthful.'

'Good,' he said. How trite can you be? he asked himself despairingly—surely he could have discovered a less pedestrian response?

Kirsty sipped her wine.

Grant watched her.

The waiter came and removed their pineapple plates. Kirsty slipped out of her waistcoat and resettled the wide sleeves and cuffs of what turned out to be a black chiffon blouse that Grant would have liked to strip straight off her.

The waiter returned with a minion pushing a carving trolley, removed the cover to display their pheasant, and began to divide it. Each of them was served with it, and everything else in sight.

'This looks marvellous,' Kirsty said, dazed but happy, as the waiter at last departed.

'Yes, doesn't it?' Grant responded automatically,

though in fact he was hardly conscious of what was on his plate at all.

Kirsty cut into her pheasant, and reverted to the Weybourne family. 'I expect Fieldy will know who you can get on to on the board of governors,' she suggested.

'Good idea. He's sure to.'

'Kevin may not have told Linda what he's up to,' Kirsty added thoughtfully, 'but I wonder if she knows he's arranging something for her? Children are often amazingly aware of what's being arranged for them, in spite of no one breathing a word. I know I always was.'

'You're right, of course. I certainly knew I was going to boarding-school, and exactly where, long before anyone sat me down and told me.'

'Oh, yes, and I knew our family was going to break up, and that Cathy was taking Julie to the weekend cottage permanently, while I stayed in Harley Street with Dad and Annabel, weeks before I was officially told.' Unexpectedly, she chuckled. 'Though I must say I am apparently much less aware of what goes on under my nose today—I seem to have entirely lost my childish extra-sensory understanding, or whatever it was.' She paused.

Grant was agonised for her. He knew what she had to be talking about, and he simply didn't know whether he wanted her to go on. He ached for her to confide in him, to tell him what she had found out about Toby and Fran—if that was what she had done—so that he could begin to comfort her, to make her understand how unimportant Toby could be in her life. On the other hand, he didn't want, at any price, to bring pain and unhappiness into their precious evening together.

'I must be thick as a plank,' she added ruminatively.

'You're not in the least thick,' Grant snapped irritably. 'No way. Don't be daft.'

'Oh, but I must be,' she told him, her eyes laughing. 'I let them both pull the wool right over my eyes, after all. My own sister—and I could have sworn I was on to all her tricks, always noticed when she was up to something. Yet I stood blindly by and watched her move out of the Old Stables and into a bedroom at the main house, and accepted without question that she was doing it only because I needed to have my bedroom back to myself, and because she was worried about disturbing me by her return late at night when I was already asleep.'

Grant sat rigid. He dared not comment, because he had no idea how much, or how little, Kirsty had discovered. He was afraid for her. Terribly afraid. And he was afraid for himself, too. At any moment she might tell him something, quite casually, that doomed him forever to be a nonentity in her life.

She was grinning at him, apparently happily. 'When I know perfectly well that Fran has never, ever, cared—or even been aware—if she disturbs anyone at any hour of the day or night, and it would equally never occur to her that I might like my bedroom to myself. No, what she was after was being able to come and go undisturbed. so that she could spend the night with Toby in his flat without me guessing. And it worked like a dream. She took me in completely.' She laughed, pulled a face at the joke against herself, and then put a forkful of pheasant into her mouth and ate it happily.

Grant stared. How had she found out? Didn't she mind? What was going on?

Before he'd pulled himself together, Kirsty added, rather as if she had reached the climax of today's biggest joke, 'It took Toby to explain it to me at lunch.' She pulled another humorous face, her eyes sparkling, and added, 'This pheasant is truly sublime. I don't think I've ever had a more splendid meal.'

'Yes, it is good,' Grant agreed absently. He took the plunge. 'What is all this about Toby and your sister, then? What's going on?'

'Oh, they've fallen in love, would you believe?' Kirsty told him blithely. 'Isn't it great?' She smiled blindingly across the table, and popped another load of pheasant into her mouth.

'Toby and your sister Fran are in love?' Grant repeated slowly, not because he was surprised by the news which, after all, had been depressing him for days on end, but because he wanted to make certain that Kirsty was genuinely happy about it. He didn't dare trust his eyes or his instincts, both of which informed him clearly that she was.

'They think they are, anyway,' she told him. 'Of course, Fran is forever in and out of love. That's why I ought to have grasped what was going on miles earlier than I did. There's nothing in the least unusual about her behaviour. But it's new for Toby, bless him. He's never really fallen hard for anyone before—I'm just praying Fran won't let him down by finding someone else suddenly.'

'You think she may?' Grant enquired, bemused.

Kirsty shrugged. 'Maybe this time it will be different. She's twenty now—perhaps she's ready to settle down. For Toby's sake I do hope so, though on past experience it's highly unlikely—but you never know. Besides, it'd be great to have Toby for a brother-in-law,' she added. 'He has his faults, but he's a huge improvement on most of Fran's hangers-on.' She began collecting the last fragments of pheasant and its accompanying apple and Cointreau sauce from the edges of her plate.

Grant had finally lost interest in the food. He wanted to dance Kirsty round the restaurant, in and out between the tables, shouting all the while at the assembled consultants and senior registrars from St Mark's, their wives and assorted girl-friends, together with other Halchester worthies dining there, the bishop and a sprinkling of cathedral clergy among them, 'She doesn't care in the least for Toby Gresham, she's mine, mine, mine forever.'

The waiter was collecting their plates, clearing the table, and summoning with a glance the loaded trolley full of the most luscious desserts.

But Grant wasn't going to go on sitting here mouthing platitudes for another second, not if he knew it.

'Do you want one of these?' he enquired, obviously expecting the answer no. Then, ashamed at trying to do her out of the rest of the meal, he added hurriedly, 'The chocolate mousse is terrific—very rich, though. Or there are the raspberries.'

Kirsty was tempted by the raspberries, which looked enticing, sitting on rounds of meringue and clotted cream. But this evening she had no problem whatever in picking up exactly what had been left unsaid, and she was as certain as Grant that what they needed most of all was to be alone together.

'I'm sure they're gorgeous, but I positively haven't another centimetre of space left, thanks all the same,' she assured him.

'Coffee, then?' he suggested. 'We could have it in my sitting-room, perhaps?'

'That would be great,' Kirsty agreed, gathering her bag and her waistcoat, and rising blissfully to her feet.

Hardly daring to believe his luck, Grant nodded to the waiter. 'Coffee in my sitting-room, thank you.'

Treading on air, both of them about ten feet above the ground, they swept out of the restaurant and into the great galleried hall. Heads turned, and eyes followed them, questioning. Knowing glances were exchanged, but none of it mattered any longer to Grant.

His sitting-room was comfortably furnished with a squashy settee and two swivel chairs, a low coffee-table between them scattered with medical periodicals, and also supporting their coffee-tray. There were low chests with bowls of flowers against the walls, and lamp-tables holding huge pottery lamps with pleated shades.

Grant switched on the two lamps, Kirsty sank into the depths of the settee and, to her immense delight—but hardly surprise—Grant sat down next to her. He leant forward to pour the coffee.

'Black, as usual?'

'Please.'

He poured, handed her her cup and saucer, proffered the bowl of *petit fours* from the tray.

'This is lovely,' she said brightly. Too brightly, she recognised the moment the words had escaped. But she didn't seem able to stop herself prattling as though her future depended on never allowing a second of silence. 'I truly think that was the most superb meal I've ever eaten.'

'To hell with the meal,' he told her. 'What I want to talk about is you. I want to hear about Toby. I knew perfectly well he was having an affair with that sister of yours, and I've been tearing myself apart. I thought you'd be upset—everyone told me you and Toby were planning to marry.'

She chuckled easily. 'You've been listening to hospital gossip,' she said. 'It's apt to be misleading, I'm afraid. The grapevine remains quaint and old-world, with distinctly Victorian attitudes. Just because Toby and I have been around together for years, they all insisted on hearing wedding-bells for the two of us.'

'Are you telling me they were entirely wrong?'

'I am. Totally wrong. Toby and I are friends, of course, we have been ever since we both came here. We got on well from the beginning, and we understood one another. In a sense I suppose you could say we provided a screen for each other, though I didn't realise that until recently—both of us like getting to know people slowly, and going around together with no strings and no panics. I'm very fond of Toby, but the fact is I know him far too well to want to live with him for the remainder of my days—I'd be far too irritated by his minor faults, for one thing. It wouldn't be fair to him.'

'Right. Point taken. So let's stop talking about Toby, and talk about us. You and me. Do you realise that I've been moronic enough all these months to make myself keep away from you because I thought you were committed to Toby? Talk about the hospital being old-world—what about me? I kept telling myself I mustn't sweep in and try to take over you as well as the consultant post he considered I'd snatched from him. I thought that would be a bad beginning—and then, of course, I didn't suppose I had a hope with you, in any case. I thought you were committed to Toby.'

'You thought you hadn't a hope with me?' Kirsty repeated. 'But that's what I thought about you. I thought you disliked me. You were so stand-offish.' Her eyes scorched his. 'What are we waiting for?' she asked.

'Nothing whatsoever. Put that damned cup down, before it spills.'

Kirsty dumped it with a clatter, and they were in one another's arms. It felt absolutely right and not in the least surprising and, while it was wildly exciting, it was equally an oasis of calm and surety.

There had never been anything like this in her life. This was what she had been waiting for all her days, to be held like this by Grant. This was what she had recognised that first time they'd met, at Northcliffe. She should have believed it then. They were two halves of one whole.

'Two halves of one whole,' she said wonderingly.

'Made for each other,' he told her tenderly, and she was kissed as no one had ever kissed her before.

'It's ridiculous,' she told him, when the world briefly ceased spinning, and she held his head in her hands and traced the line of his brows. 'I feel so safe like this, as if nothing could ever go wrong again, because we have each other.'

'Me, too.' He kissed the tips of her fingers.

Her eyes blazing, she looked straight into his. 'Perhaps we're both quite mad, but it feels wonderful, and I don't believe it will ever go away.'

'It won't, I promise you. We've found each other—after a lot of quite unnecessary hanging around and muddling about, I can't imagine why, now, when it's all so simple. And we're staying together. Agreed?' The dark eyes she treasured probed hers, and though he threw the question at her like a challenge, the eyes held anxiety in their depths.

'Agreed,' she repeated, and her grey eyes held no doubt or uncertainty. 'I love you,' she told him, and now it was her arms that were strong and sure. 'Forever, I'm afraid.'

'Forever,' he repeated, and now his eyes met hers with love and tenderness in their depths. 'My own true love, forever.'

The telephone on the coffee-table buzzed demandingly, and Grant swore with a fury that made Kirsty smile even as her heart sank.

'Wouldn't you *know*?' she asked.

He picked up the telephone, and snapped 'Yes?'

The telephone quacked relentlessly, and Grant said yes and no at intervals, until finally, 'Right, Quentin, I'll be over.' He put the telephone down and did some more swearing, only to break off abruptly. 'Look, my love, wait for me here, will you? Please. I—I shouldn't be more than half an hour. Could you—would you, just wait here for me? Do you think? And I'll be back.'

'I'll wait,' she said. 'For as long as it takes. Always.'

A years supply of Mills & Boon romances — absolutely free!

Would you like to win a years supply of heartwarming and passionate romances? Well, you can and they're FREE! All you have to do is complete the word puzzle below and send it to us by 29th February 1996. The first 5 correct entries picked out of the bag after that date will win a years supply of Mills & Boon romances (six books every month—worth over £100). What could be easier?

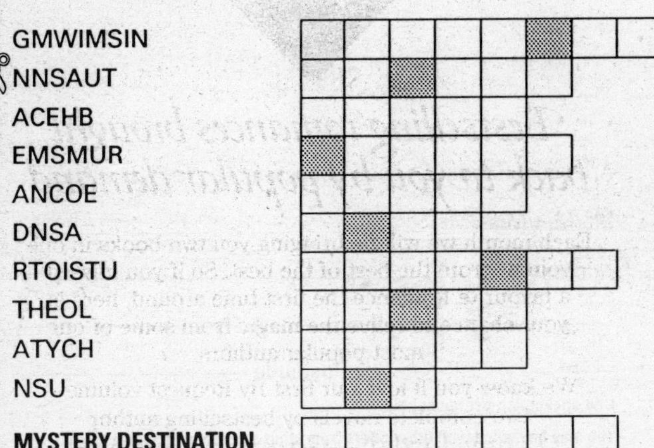

Please turn over for details on how to enter

How to enter

Simply sort out the jumbled letters to make ten words all to do with being on holiday. Enter your answers in the grid, then unscramble the letters in the shaded squares to find out our mystery holiday destination.

After you have completed the word puzzle and found our mystery destination, don't forget to fill in your name and address in the space provided below and return this page in an envelope (you don't need a stamp). Competition ends 29th February 1996.

Mills & Boon Romance Holiday Competition
FREEPOST
P.O. Box 344
Croydon
Surrey
CR9 9EL

Are you a Reader Service Subscriber? Yes ❑ No ❑

Ms/Mrs/Miss/Mr ______________________________

Address ______________________________

____

______________________________ Postcode ______________________________

One application per household.

You may be mailed with other offers from other reputable companies as a result of this application. If you would prefer not to receive such offers, please tick box. ❑

COMP495
B